George Perkins Clinton

Orange Rust of Raspberry and Blackberry

George Perkins Clinton

Orange Rust of Raspberry and Blackberry

ISBN/EAN: 9783337419035

Printed in Europe, USA, Canada, Australia, Japan

Cover: Foto ©Andreas Hilbeck / pixelio.de

More available books at **www.hansebooks.com**

UNIVERSITY OF ILLINOIS,

Agricultural Experiment Station.

CHAMPAIGN, DECEMBER, 1893.

BULLETIN NO. 29.

CONTENTS—ORANGE RUST IN RASPBERRIES AND BLACKBERRIES.
A NEW FACTOR IN SCIENTIFIC AGRICULTURE.

---

*ORANGE RUST OF RASPBERRY AND BLACKBERRY.

For the past twenty-five years notes have appeared in various agricultural and horticultural publications of this country of a fungus occurring on raspberries and blackberries, which, on account of the bright orange colored spores produced on the leaves, has been uniformly known as " orange rust." So marked and so persistent is the action upon these berry plants, its " hosts, " of this lowly organized parasitic plant that it is recognized as one of the most destructive of what are known as parasitic fungi.

To botanists this fungus has been known since the earlier part of the present century, when it was first mentioned as occurring in Kamtchatka, and soon after, in Carolina of this country. A glance at "Distribution " in the Appendix shows that it is quite widely spread over the eastern part of the United States. In some localities, however, it is much more abundant than in others. Mention of it has not been found as occurring further west than Nebraska, and Dr. Harkness, in a letter,

---

*The writer wishes to acknowledge his indebtedness to Professor Burrill, who first suggested the possible relationship of *Caeoma nitens* and *Puccinia Peckiana*, and at whose suggestion the investigation of their life histories was undertaken. To various botanists who have responded to our letters of inquiry, thanks are also due. Reference to articles is made in the text by giving author's name and date of publication; but such references may be found more fully given under " Literature," in the Appendix. After the above paper had been written for publication, an article by Tranzschel, published in *Hedwigia*, was received. By artificial infection, this writer so completely verifies the results that we have obtained that his experiments have been added to the paper, and proper credit has been given.

states that he has never collected it in California. It is not at all improbable, however, that it may be found further west. Reports give it as occurring in our most southern states, and from them it extends beyond our northern limits into Canada. In Europe and Asia, while not so numerously reported, it has been found over a large range of territory and is said to be quite common in some of the northern stations.

So far as known this fungus has limited its ravages to the genus Rubus. Both cultivated and wild species are freely attacked, and of the former quite a number of varieties have been reported as more or less injured, of which the Kittatinny is perhaps one of the worst affected. In this region the Snyder seems usually to be quite exempt from attack, although elsewhere reported as more or less infected. In the Appendix is given a list of species so far found to be attacked.

The fungus shows its first signs of appearance in early spring, varying slightly in time as the weather is favorable or not to the growth of its host. In this locality it can first be detected during the latter part of April or the first of May. As soon as the leaves are fairly started in their development, and before they are unfolded, what is known as the spermagonial stage can be seen. The spermagonia resemble small stalked glands thickly covering both sides of the leaf, and at first are so deceiving in their appearance as to be mistaken for glands naturally belonging to the leaf. As the leaves mature, the spermagonia become more distinct, and while usually found covering the leaves of the affected plant, are sometimes variously limited in their distribution. Some leaves, usually the upper, may be affected, and others entirely free; even some of the leaflets of a single leaf may show this stage while others do not. Nor is it an uncommon occurrence to find definitely affected patches of an individual leaflet sharply marked off from the remaining apparently healthy parts. About two or three weeks after the first appearance of the spermagonia, the second, or aecidium stage becomes noticeable, showing as concealed, slightly elevated spots thickly covering the under surface of the leaf. The rapid growth of these soon ruptures the epidermis above each bed of spores, and they then show as bright orange colored masses. About this time the spermagonia have reached their maximum development. So far as observed the aecidium stage is limited to those leaves or parts of the leaf that were affected by the spermagonia, although all parts affected with spermagonia do not necessarily produce the former. The aecidium stage is confined almost entirely to the lower surface of the leaf, rarely slightly affecting the margin on the upper side. It is also found, in rare cases, on the stems. It reaches its maximum development here during the first part of June, and during the latter part of the month gradually disappears until only isolated cases can rarely be found during the first of July. Some writers mention it as occurring again during the autumn months. Brunk (1890) claims to have found it in Maryland as late as the middle of October, and writes that in the extreme southern states he has found specimens in

December.   It has been found by the writer during the spring and early summer only.

The fungus is found on the leaves of old and new shoots, and is usually so vigorous in its spore development that it utterly destroys the usefulness of the affected leaves.   These fall off in time, and if the fungus has not so far impaired the vitality of the plant as to prevent further development, the subsequent growth of branches with unaffected leaves may help repair the damage.   Frequently, however, especially in young shoots, the canes, stripped of their leaves, hindered in growth, fail to overcome the damage, and so die.   Since it is also a fact that a plant once infected is quite certain of attack each succeeding year, it is usually only a matter of time before the most vigorous of plants are rendered worthless.   Sometimes the presence of only the spermagonial stage is sufficient seriously to affect the efficiency of young shoots. Horticultural papers sometimes contain notices of localities in which blackberries and raspberries in general are so seriously affected by this disease as to render their cultivation unprofitable, if not impossible. The same plants or patches being annually subject to attack early led many to suppose that the fungus must be perennial in its host, a fact which was first publicly demonstrated by Newcombe (1891), who found mycelium in microscopical sections taken from different parts of affected plants.

This perennial nature of the fungus makes successful prevention of the disease exceedingly difficult.   Various methods of treatment have been made, of which probably only one has given any uniformly good results, that of digging up and destroying all affected plants as soon as signs of disease were manifested.   Spraying has been tried to see if any good could be accomplished.   With the mycelium perennial in the host, the good in this case must be in preventing the spread of the disease to unaffected plants, and then only under conditions depending upon the life history of the fungus.   If the aecidiospores germinate upon the leaves of Rubus to produce another stage of development, then spraying at the proper season should be beneficial in this direction.   As the indications are that the above supposition is correct, spraying with Bordeaux mixture as soon as the aecidiospores begin to show, preceded by a thorough cutting out of plants as soon as signs of the disease are manifested, should, in a few seasons, eradicate this disease.   As the spores in germination seem to gain entrance on the under side of the leaf, it would be especially necessary in spraying to wet that side.   The fungus has also some natural enemies that are of slight use in destroying its spores.   Among these may be mentioned the larvae of certain insects, which feed quite greedily on the spores, and *Tuberculina persicina*, a fungus which occurs frequently as a parasite on the sori.

Having stated that a plant once attacked by this disease is perennially subject to it, let us see why this is so.   This will lead us to consider the vegetative stage of the fungus, or what is technically known as the mycelium.

MYCELIUM.

The bright, orange colored patches on the under side of the leaves are made up entirely of spores, or the reproductive part of the fungus. To produce these there must be a vegetative system; just as to produce the fruit of the blackberry there must be the root, the stem, and the leaf. This vegetative, or mycelial stage is concealed entirely within the plant, and in this fungus, contrary to the usual rule of its family, is quite extensively developed. To show this, microscopical sections of the affected plants are necessary. From those made of variously affected parts the following facts have been learned concerning this stage of the fungus: Such sections reveal mycelial threads present from the upper parts of the roots running through the stem up into the uppermost leaves showing signs of affection. That is, we may take any affected leaf, make sections of its blade, its petiole, the junction of petiole to branch or main shoot, and so down the stem to the perennial part, and even somewhat into the root itself, and in all the sections find the mycelium. Frequently plants are found in which the new shoots are affected but the old ones are free. In such cases the mycelium is found in the former only. The canes of raspberries and blackberries are biennial, and, so far as personal inspection goes, unless these are infected during their first year they can not be the second; and if they are affected the first year, they are quite sure to be the next. This is easily explained by the fact that the mycelium follows young growing cells, and cannot penetrate tissue to any extent after it has matured. Sections of very young canes of the diseased plants show that they contain mycelium, and that in such it follows quite closely the point of growth. In such sections, fungus threads have been traced from the stem into the scale-like leaves protecting it, and into the ordinary leaves before they have become differentiated into blade and petiole. Sections of roots, except in the neighborhood of the merging of root and stem, do not show the mycelium. Now, from the above, one can see how a single plant can have both new and old stems affected and free, illustrations of which are sometimes met. In such a case the unaffected canes come from underground parts into which the mycelium failed to penetrate when they were young, and so was shut out; and the affected ones come from where the mycelium had gained entrance. The above facts also prove that the first infection of a plant must be through the shoots when very young and easy of penetration. The plants present this condition during late fall and early spring. As illustrating the perennial nature of the fungus, and method of infection, the following experiment is given: In 1892 eighteen plants were marked, of which ten were affected with this Caeoma and eight were free. In 1893 these were examined again, and the ten diseased in 1892 were found to be in the same condition, and the eight healthy ones of the year before were so still, except in one case. This plant was affected only on the new, very young canes, showing that through them the fungus gained entrance.

The structure of this vegetative stage, when examined, is found to consist of two parts—mycelial threads and haustoria. The function of the former is, evidently, to carry the fungus to different parts of the plant; and so the threads are found between the cell walls, quite often in the spaces where three or more cells come together. In transverse sections of the plant these show as cut ends, while in longitudinal sections they can frequently be traced for quite a distance. In such cases they appear as hyaline filaments of varying diameter, having definite cell walls, and, according to age, more or less protoplasm. From these spring the haustoria, similar but very short threads. The haustorium pierces the cell wall by a narrow neck and inside the cell enlarges into a body with a more or less knobbed end, the function of an haustorium being to supply nourishment necessary for the growth of the mycelium. The fungus filaments are not found distributed irregularly through the plant, but are limited to certain localities. In the root and root-like part they are found between the parenchyma cells of the cortex in the vicinity of the cambium. The abundance of starch in these cells makes it necessary that very thin sections be made, which show best when stained with an alcoholic solution of potassium iodide and iodine, thereby coloring the starch grains blue and the fungus a yellowish green. In cells containing haustoria their effect upon the amount of starch in very evident (*Plate 3, fig. 12*). As a rule, in this part of the plant, the largest and most knobbed of the haustoria have been found. In the stems the mycelium is found in the pith, mostly between the smaller cells near the fibro-vascular bundles. The leaves have the mycelium entering them when quite young, and the interstices of the parenchyma cells afford its abode. In young shoots the mycelium is not so limited to particular localities, occurring occasionally among the parenchyma cells of the bark, and even among the outermost cells of the bundles not yet fully developed.

The appearance of the mycelium depends somewhat on its age. When young it is more conspicuous, but when old it loses its protoplasm and acquires an occasional septum. The haustoria are at first simple threads extending half way or more across the cell. They soon begin, by coiling or twisting, to form an enlarged, knotted end. This possibly may be due to the effort of the haustorium to come into more intimate contact with its food particles. Sometimes two haustoria are found in the same cell, and not infrequently have there been seen signs of union of these (*Plate 3, fig. 3, 4, 7*). This, however, is to be interpreted as nothing more than an accidental occurrence.

Late in April a more conspicuous gathering of mycelium in special places just beneath the epidermis of the leaves is noticeable, and then begins the formation of the first fruiting stage of the fungus, or the spermagonia.

SPERMAGONIA.

Transverse sections through one of these mycelial groups at this time show the threads as an indefinite mass chiefly in cross section. The threads begin to grow upward between the lateral union of contiguous epidermal cells, forcing the cells apart and upward as a slight papilla. Sections now show the mycelium in these papillae more in longitudinal view as closely packed, septate threads, and the epidermis above the infected spot is seen as two large cells, forced above the level of the surrounding cells at their juncture with each other, and separated from each other at their bases by the intervening mass of mycelium (*Plate 2, fig. 1, 2*). According to Richards (1893) further growth so pushes against the interior walls of these elevated cells as to cause them to collapse, and the cells become filled with mycelium. The upright threads, so closely crowded together as to form a sort of false tissue, having reached their growth, begin to cut off from their upper free ends numerous small oval bodies. These are known as spermatia, and when entirely formed occupy about the upper third of the spermagonium. When they have been formed in sufficient numbers, the epidermal covering becomes punctured, and they ooze out on the exterior of the leaf as a small viscid drop.

The function of these spore-like bodies is not definitely known. Some botanists consider such as male elements concerned in the fertilization of the aecidium stage of fungi. The function of somewhat similar bodies found in lichens has led to this view, and, while rather generally accepted, there seems to be no direct evidence that these so-called spermatia are really such. Some have thought that these bodies effect fertilization of the mycelium, while others have held that each aecidiospore may be fertilized by a spermatium, as spermatia are frequently seen adhering to the spores. The fact that spermagonia are generally produced with the aecidium stage, and that both are borne on the same mycelium suggests, at least, intimate relationship. Other botanists have discarded the idea that these were at all sexual elements, and declare that they are merely conidial stages of the fungus, and that the so-called spermatia are conidiospores. Plowright, holding this view, claims to have produced a yeast-like germination of these bodies in sweetened water. A similar germination was also previously claimed by Cornu. In culture experiments with the spermatia of this fungus, such a method of reproduction has been noticed, but satisfaction was not had that such did not contain yeast fungi. The chief objection to the view that these are conidial bodies is the special use they could have, since they are generally produced in connection with the aecidium stage whose spores have an almost similar function. Winter merely says that the physiological significance of the spermatia is not yet surely made out. Be their use what it may, about the time of their maximum development the signs of a second spore stage become visible to the naked eye.

CAEOMA, OR AECIDIUM STAGE.

This, known as "orange rust," is the most conspicuous stage, on account of being seen externally and because of the bright color of the spores. Like the spermagonia, it has its origin in the mycelium of the leaf, only this time the mycelium begins to form in masses on the lower side of the leaf. Here is produced a more extended development of filaments. From these arises a compact mass of threads divided with septa, in a basipetal manner, into distinct cells. The distal cells gradually become rounded at their septal unions, and are less securely fastened together. Their walls also become minutely verruculose, and, though hyaline, are given an apparent color by the endochrome which with the protoplasm fills the cell. The aecidiospores thus mature, and separate into distinct bodies. These being formed now just beneath the epidermis, the strain on it becomes too great and a rupture takes place. The epidermis above the sorus soon wears away and the golden spot, until now seen indefinitely through the epidermis, shows as bright orange. The spores when fully matured vary from elliptical or oblong to sub-globose, and usually measure 12 to 24 by 18 to 32 microns. Their thin, hyaline exospore is finely covered with minute tubercules. Their orange color is due to the presence of a considerable amount of endochrome.

If, soon after these spores are mature, they are put in a moist place germination takes place. In watching this under the microscope, the following has been found most useful: A glass ring, the diameter of the cover glass and about a quarter of an inch high, is fastened to the glass slip by means of vaseline. In a drop of sterilized water on the cover glass are dusted a few of the mature spores. This is inverted and fastened on the top of the ring by means of vaseline previously placed on its edges. If for any reason one finds the water drop too deep for focusing on its free surface, this can be prevented by washing the cover before use with caustic potash. Cultures thus made can be examined through all stages of spore germination without fear of evaporation. Mature, fresh spores often show signs of germination within three hours after being placed in water. The first sign is a small swelling appearing on the side of the spore. The contents of the spore, surrounded by the endospore, have pierced the exospore through a small opening, and have swollen into a small hyaline body. This gradually lengthens by apical growth into filamentous form, and then the endochrome appears in the tube as small colored globules. The growth of the tube is about the same for eight or ten hours, when it has reached a length three or four times the diameter of the spore. All this time the protoplasm has been disappearing from the spore and entering the germ tube. The protoplasm of the spore at first becomes less dense, then vacuoles appear, and the contents are gradually limited to the region of the germ pore.

The spore is thus emptied in about eight hours, but the germ tube keeps on growing, and gradually becomes empty at its base. As the protoplasm recedes from the lower part of the tube, an occasional septum may be formed. Growth is practically stopped only by the exhaustion of the protoplasm, and usually lasts for two or three days after the first signs of germination, the length of the tubes at this period frequently being eight or more times the diameter of the spore. The germ tubes are mostly of a uniform diameter, with the tips sometimes slightly narrowed. They usually present a slightly flexuous, rather than a rigid, straight growth. Upon some occasions movement of the protoplasmic granules can be seen in the germ tubes. Occasionally germination presents anomalies in the shape of suddenly enlarged or of flexuous tips, and in a single case branching has been seen, but never more than a single developed germ tube has been found to a spore.

Such being the characters presented in artificial germination, in what manner should we expect these spores to act when infecting their hosts? Botanists have proved that such summer spores gain entrance into plants by the growth of the germ tubes into the stomates of the epidermis and so into the parenchyma tissue of the leaves. This being the case it is left for decision whether with these germinating spores the blackberry and raspberry leaves are used for further development, or whether, as is so often the case, some other entirely different plants have been chosen. The indications being that the former was the case, artificial growth on the leaves was undertaken. In both raspberry and blackberry, the stomates are almost entirely confined to the under side of the leaf, some few being found on the margins of the upper side. In the former, too, the lower surface is so covered by hairs as to afford considerable difficulty in examining the epidermis. So blackberry leaves on a small shoot were moistened on their lower surface and then dusted with spores. The shoot was then placed in a moist chamber and left for twenty-four hours. Examination of the leaves was then made under the microscope. The epidermis of these leaves sticks so closely to the parenchyma cells that it cannot be satisfactorily removed. The leaf itself is too opaque for examination under high powers. It was necessary, therefore, carefully to soak pieces of the leaf in hot caustic potash, wash, and squeeze slightly under the cover glass before the surface of the epidermis could be examined. Such a process, however, is likely to wash off any spores that may be on the surface of the leaf. Under such circumstances were found, on one occasion, spores that showed signs of entering the stomates (*Plate 4, fig. 22*). These spores presented characters never seen in mere water cultures; for, after they had sent out an ordinary tube about three times the diameter of the spore, it suddenly became considerably narrowed; and in several cases this narrowed part was found between the guard cells of the stomates, showing, at least, that the fungus could gain entrance in this way. No germ tubes were ever found piercing through the epidermis itself. The experiment of inoculating a healthy plant, kept indoors, was also tried; but as about the time results from this could be expected the plant died, evidence in either direction was wanting.

Since these spores germinate readily as soon as mature, and probably infect blackberries and raspberries through their leaves, it might seem that they were means of spreading the aecidium stage from plant to plant. But when we consider that this stage is limited to spring and that no plant or parts of a plant become diseased except those early showing its signs, such an inference becomes impossible, and we are led to inquire to what does this stage give rise? This brings to our consideration what is known as alternation of spore forms.

ALTERNATION OF SPORE FORMS.

The fact that the aecidiospores soon lose their power of germination, coupled with the knowledge that such spores have been proved in numerous cases to be merely summer stages of more advanced forms, has suggested, with almost certainty, that this fungus has other spore stages in its life history not now recognized as belonging to it. Botanists have, therefore, suggested different forms as the mature stage, basing their opinions on more or less superficial observations. Let us see what evidence there is that such are advanced stages of this fungus.

Melampsora. Dietel gives the following species of Melampsora and Caeoma that different investigators have connected with each other by culture experiments.

Melampsora Salicis capreae, (Pers.) and *Caeoma Euonymi,* (Gmel.) —Rostrup.

Melampsora Hartigii, (Thüm.) and *Caeoma Ribesii,* Lk.— Rostrup.

Melampsora aecidioides, (DC.) and *Caeoma Mercurialis,* (Pers.) —Plowright.

Melampsora Tremulae, Tul. and $\left\{\begin{array}{l}\textit{Caeoma Mercurialis,} \text{ (Pers.)} \\ \textit{Caeoma pinitorquum,} \text{ A. Br.}\end{array}\right\}$ —Rostrup.

Melampsora Tremulae, Tul. and *Caeoma Laricis,* (Westd.)—Hartig.

Melampsora Populina, Jacq. and *Caeoma Laricis,* (Westd.)—Hartig.

Plowright also made cultures to duplicate the above results, but was successful in only the case attributed to him. These results indicate a close relationship between Melampsora and Caeoma, and suggest that the mature form of the Caeoma we are considering might be found among the species of Melampsora. So far as is known no culture experiments have been made along this line. The fact that this Caeoma is so common would indicate that the teleutoform was not rare, and this again would suggest the Melampsora on Populus or Salix as the most probable one; but, apparently, the above investigators have found both of these species connected with entirely different species of Caeoma. Rathay also claims to have found *Melampsora populina* as connected with *Aecidium clematidis,* and this, taken with other conflict-

ing results in the above list, makes it quite improbable that all species of
Caeoma will be found connected with Melampsora as the mature stage.

Phragmidium. Another genus with which some botanists have
suggested connection with this Caeoma is Phragmidium, especially with
the species *Ph. Rubi.* The facts that in this genus all three spore forms
may occur on the same host species, and that in some, *Ph. mucronatum,*
the aecidium stage has gross resemblance to *C. nitens,* together with the
further facts that *Ph. Rubi* and *C. nitens* are found on the same hosts
and frequently in the same localities, seem to be the chief points in
favor of considering them as forms of the same thing. Perhaps, too,
the fact that the aecidium form of *Ph. Rubi* is wanting or little known
in some localities has had much to do with suggesting the connection.
These, however, are too general points to be of definite value in proving
connection of the forms. Let us see what more specific points will
indicate. As to structure, we find some difference between the
ordinary aecidium stage of Phragmidium and this Caeoma, for in the
former paraphyses surrounding the sori are characteristic, while in the
latter there is no evidence of them. We find no recorded cases of both
forms occurring commonly on the same individual host, as one might
expect if they were related. Then, in this locality at least, the failure
to find this Caeoma after the first of July, while the collections of *Ph.
Rubi* have not been made earlier than September, is also against their
connection, as two months between the disappearance of an aecidium and
the appearance of an uredo form is too long a time for which to account.
Lastly, most European botanists have considered this Caeoma as distinct
from the Phragmidium, especially since Krieger has found and described
an aecidium form that corresponds to the normal type of such stages of
Phragmidium, and which is now accepted as the first stage of *Ph.
Rubi.* Since the aecidium and uredo forms of Phragmidium are frequently so similar, it is not at all unlikely that in this country the earlier
stages of *Ph. Rubi* have occasionally been classed indefinitely under
the uredo form.

Puccinia. Still another genus, Puccinia, has been named as having connection with *C. nitens.* In 1885 Burrill suggested that a relationship might exist between *Caeoma nitens* and *Puccinia Peckiana,*
as both were found in Illinois on the same hosts. Our study of these
fungi has led to the belief that this is the most probable explanation.
Let us see what is the life history of the latter fungus, and then determine what evidence there is to offer it as the mature form of the
Caeoma.

In this vicinity the fungus, *P. Peckiana,* makes its appearance on
leaves of raspberry and blackberry about the first of July, and has been
collected on them as late as September. While the fungus usually occurs
on the under side of the leaf, an occasional sorus is found on the margin of
the upper surface. The sori are so small as generally to escape attention when the leaf is not badly affected, and sometimes are to be recog-

nized only by aid of a magnifier. They frequently occur in small, isolated clusters, but often the leaf is abundantly covered with them, and then the peculiar mottled green and yellow appearance of the upper surface serves as a ready aid of detection to the trained eye. Cross sections of affected leaves show mycelium in different parts running between the parenchyma cells, but much more abundant toward the lower surface. Plants known never to have been affected with the Caeoma show mycelium confined to the leaf. The mycelium gives rise directly to the teleutospores; and, so far, these only have been found. They are formed in the usual method: by accumulation of mycelium near the under surface; formation of erect, fertile branches; differentiation into spores; and eventual rupture by these of the epidermis. The mature spores are quite characteristic in their appearance. They reach an average size of 22 to 27 by 36 to 45 microns. The cell walls are of a reddish brown color, and of nearly uniform thickness. The spores vary considerably as to shape, especially as the front and side views of the same spore are not exactly the same. Usually, however, the apical cell is somewhat triangular, with apex covered with several hyaline papillae. Occasionally these papillae have been seen sparsely covering the whole cell. The basal cell is frequently quadrangular, with the short, hyaline, fugacious pedicle at one corner and the other formed by a few hyaline papillae.

Attempts at germination of these spores have been made at various times of the year, except in spring, but were successful only on one occasion. About the middle of September lately gathered spores were placed in water, and, failing to show signs of germination at the end of the third day, the slide was laid aside and not examined until the spores had been a week in the water. It was then found that a few spores had sent out germ tubes (*Plate 4, fig. 24–29*). The endospore pierced the exospore through a small opening, and immediately enlarged into the natural diameter of the promycelium. Apical growth of this took place until it had reached a length two or three times the diameter of the spore. This was about sufficient to empty the cell of its contents. Both apical and basal cells were found to germinate, though but a single tube was produced from a cell, and no example was found of both cells of the same spore germinating. The germination ceased before there was any evidence of the formation of promycelial spores. The germination of the spores at this time of the year suggests that they infect their host through some other place than the leaves.

So much for the life history of this fungus, but how may the phenomena it presents, together with those of the Caeoma, be interpreted? These will be considered in the following paragraphs on Distribution, Hosts, Life Histories, and Artificial Infection.

Distribution. While the distribution of this Puccinia has not been apparently so widespread, or so frequently reported as in the case of the Caeoma, still it has been found in the same regions only with the

latter.   Under "Hosts" of the Appendix are given the localities in which
these have been found.   The effect of the former on its hosts is so incon-
spicuous, especially when compared with that of the latter, that there is
no doubt that its range will be more widely extended when a careful
search is made for it.   This conclusion is based on experience in this
locality; for, while here the Caeoma had always been considered common, the Puccinia was not, until a careful search revealed it to be at
least as common, if not more so, than the former fungus.   In five
localities watched during the past three years both forms have appeared
abundantly.

Hosts.   Naturally enough, the Puccinia having been less frequently
seen, the number of host species it occupies will be found to be less, as
is shown in the Appendix; but such as it does attack are the same as
those upon which the Caeoma occurs.   Until recently only one was reported from Europe, but it is the same as that upon which the Caeoma
was first reported over seventy years ago.   In this vicinity they
leave the same host species exactly, and on the cultivated plants both
have been found on the variety known as the Kittatiny.   In a patch of
these affected with both forms, neither was seen on an occasional Snyder
growing there.   Not only are they found occurring in the same locality
and on the same species, but the writer has recorded hundreds of examples where they occurred on the same individual.   This is forcibly
shown by an experiment, given in detail in the Appendix, to determine
if they were common on the same individual.   In early May, as soon
as the spermagonia began to show, all the affected plants were marked
in a place about two rods wide and twenty long.   Later, in June, when
the aecidium form began to appear, these thirty-four plants were again
examined and it was found that all had developed the aecidium stage.
In July, they were examined a third time, and *Puccinia Peckiana*
was found on all except two or three plants; that is, about 90 per cent
were affected.   In these exceptions the lower leaves, those most likely
to become affected, had all dropped off.   As some might think that the
occurrence of the Caeoma and the Puccinia on the same plant was accidental, a check was had by examining for the Puccinia plants not affected
by the Caeoma.   Such plants of course would not be so likely to
become infected unless they were close to those affected by the Caeoma.
These twenty plants were chosen at random from those near and away
from the marked plants.   Of these, thirteen were free, and seven affected,
or 65 per cent free.   The seven having the Puccinia were all within
three feet of plants affected with the Caeoma; while of those free, ten
were from one to several rods from the nearest marked plant.   Cases
have also been found in which the same leaf had sori of both not the
twentieth of an inch apart (*Plate 1, fig. 2*).   The fact that the Puccinia is not uniformly found with the Caeoma is easily explained.   The
two forms are produced from entirely different myceliums, and as the
aecidium form is so destructive to the leaves it attacks, they are fre-

quently destroyed and have fallen off before the time of appearance of the teleutoform.

Life Histories. Another thing that forcibly strikes one as to the connection of these fungi is their time occurrence. The Caeoma, abundantly producing spores during June, gradually disappears just as the Puccinia begins to appear on the same hosts in early July. As the aecidiospores, though germinating abundantly, do not produce the aecidium stage, what could be more natural than that mature spore forms, occurring on the same hosts and at the proper interval of time, should be connected with them? Again, what other influence can be had when the Puccinia spores are found mostly on the lower leaves, where the aecidiospores can best fall from the affected leaves above? We have found several cases of a leaf unusually affected by Puccinia that was just beneath a Caeoma infected leaf. Again, these aecidiospores gain entrance into their host through the stomates, and, as our culture experiments indicate, through those of Rubus; the stomates of our raspberries and blackberries are found on the under side and margins of the upper side of the leaves; the Puccinia sori are found only in these places. But if the germ tubes of the aecidiospores enter through the stomates and these are on the under side, what avail is it even if the Caeoma affected leaves are above? The Caeoma affects the earliest leaves. Many leaves on lower, unaffected branches are beginning to unfold when these aecidiospores are mature. These young leaves are folded together conduplicately, usually with the margins upward. The lower surface is thus exposed and is not yet well protected by hairs. This is undoubtedly the time when most of the leaves are entered by the Puccinia producing agent, a fact that is further emphasized when we find that leaves of the raspberry affected by the Puccinia are not usually so hairy beneath as those that are free. The production of these hairs has been lessened by the presence of the fungus in the leaf tissues, and to effect this the leaf must have become infected before the hairs were fully developed. In examining the epidermis of leaves at about the time the Puccinia began to appear, threads of mycelium could frequently be seen beneath the stomates, and in a few cases what looked like the broken end of an upright thread seemed to be coming up between the guard cells (*Plate 4, fig. 30*). We have, however, never been able to trace this to an aecidiospore. Lastly, the Puccinia spores germinating in fall, possibly in spring also, when infection of mature leaves would be useless and when the young underground sprouts are in condition for infection, seems to indicate that the Puccinia enters the plant through these underground parts. Since the spores of the Puccinia fall off from the leaf very easily, it being impossible to find them on old leaves in spring, the spores might very easily be washed down against the young shoots. But if the sporidia of the Puccinia stage enter these young shoots or their parts they do not give rise to the Puccinia producing mycelium, for this is limited to the leaves. Why not, then, give rise to the mycelium of this Caeoma?

Artificial Infection. But after all, the chief proof of connection of two forms is by artificially producing the one from the other. Our experiments along this line have been fewer and unsatisfactory. The plants to be experimented with were transplanted in spring and died before inoculation could be made, or before time for judging of its effects. It is hoped to continue experiments in this direction. What one might call natural infection seems to be furnished by those examples where badly Puccinia affected leaves appeared just beneath a Caeoma infected leaf. However, this weak point in our evidence is strengthened by the experiments of Tranzschel (1893), whose article came to hand after this paper had been written, but the results of whose experiments are appended to this paragraph. In 1892 and 1893 he undertook infection of plants of *Rubus Saxatilis* with the aecidiospores of *Caeoma nitens.* His experiments were carried on at the botanical gardens of the University of St. Petersburg. June 18, 1893, plants both in and out of doors had the spores placed on the leaves of their young shoots, and the 12th of July the first teleutospores of *Puccinia Peckiana* were found on the plant kept indoors. The next day they were found on one of the two plants placed outdoors, and by the 24th the plants experimented with had a number of leaves badly affected. He also reports that in one locality especially examined the Puccinia was common on plants previously affected with the aecidium stage of the Caeoma.

CONCLUSIONS.

From what has been presented, the following conclusions may be given:

1. The so called *Caeoma nitens,* a widespread and very destructive fungus of raspberries and blackberries, has been proved to possess a perennial mycelium, which probably first gains entrance into its hosts through very young underground shoots.

2. This mycelium, following the growing parts of the plant, in early spring, gives rise to spermagonial, and soon after to aecidium stages, the function of the former being as yet unproved.

3. The aecidiospores, by immediate germination, give rise to a more mature spore form, which is in no way connected with the original mycelium.

4. These aecidiospores produce this form by infecting the host through the stomates of the leaves, and evidence now proves *Rubus* as the host infected, and *Puccinia Peckiana* as the teleutoform thus produced.

5. *Puccinia Peckiana,* produced on the under side of leaves of raspberry and blackberry, germinates its spores in the fall, and possibly in early spring, and probably enters its hosts through young underground shoots.

6. The two facts that the mycelium of the Puccinia is limited to the leaves, and that the mycelium of the Caeoma is found throughout the plant suggest that the mycelium of the aecidium stage has its origin from the germinating Puccinia spores.

APPENDIX.

NOMENCLATURE.

*1820, *Caeoma interstitiale,* Schlechtendal. Horae physicae Berolinenses, p. 96.

1822, *Aecidium nitens,* Schweinitz. Synop. Fungi Car., p. 69, n. 458.

1825, *Caeoma (Aecidium) luminatum,* Link. In Species Plantarum, T. VI, P. II, p. 61, n. 166.

1825, *Caeoma interstitiale.* Link in Species Plantarum, T. VI, P. II, p. 32, n. 89.

1827, *Uredo interstitialis,* Schl. Sprengel in Systema vegetabilium, V. IV, p. 574.

1831, *Caeoma (Aecidium) luminatum,* Schweinitz. North American Fungi, p. 293, n. 2887. Printed in 1834.

*1859, *Uredo lucida,* Dietrich. Blicke in die Cryptogamenwelt der Ostseeprovinzen, Abth. II, p. 492.

1869, *Puccinia Peckiana,* Howe. 23 Rep. Bot., N. Y. State Museum, p. 57. Printed in 1872.

1870, *Puccinia tripustulata,* Peck. 24 Rep. Bot., N. Y. State Museum, p. 91. Printed in 1872.

1893, *Puccinia interstitiale* (Schlechd.), Tranzschel. Hedwigia, Heft. 5, p. 257.

So far as can be made out from the above and other references, the the history of the fungus is as follows:

In 1817, Ehrenberg, while on a journey, made some collections of fungi in Kamtchatka. Schlechtendal, in 1820, while working over the Caeoma of this collection, came across one on *Rubus arcticus,* which he described as a new species under the title of *Caeoma interstitiale.* Two years later, Schweinitz, of America, in publishing the fungi collected in Carolina, also described as new a fungus on *Rubus strigosus,* to which he gave the name, *Aecidium nitens.* In 1825, Link, writing up descriptions of known fungi, gave both Schlechtendal's fungus and Schweinitz' fungus, in the latter case, however, placing the fungus in the genus Caeoma and retaining Aecidium as a subgenus. Then, without authority as recognized to-day, he rejected the specific term applied by Schweinitz and substituted "luminatum" for the same. When Sprengel published the *Systema Vegetabilium,* in 1827, he recognized the Asiatic and American forms as the same, for he gave *Aecidium nitens* Schw. as a synonym for *Uredo interstitialis,* Schl. Schweinitz, in his second publication, in 1831, accepted the specific name as exchanged by Link, but added his own name as the authority. According to Tranzschel the fungus was again described

---

* References marked thus (*) I have not been able to examine personally.

as new in 1859 by Dietrich, who used the name *Uredo lucida.* Streinz (1862), in his *Nomenclator fungorum,* placed the forms of Schweinitz and Schlechtendal together, recognizing "interstitialis" as the specific term; and Oudemans (1891), in a note in *Hedwigia,* again called attention to their identity. Some considerable confusion has been caused by Karsten (1879), who described this Caeoma as the Aecidium form of *Phragmidium Rubi.* Winter (1884), used this description of Karsten's, but stated that he had never seen this stage of Phragmidium, but in 1885 he evidently recognized the Caeoma as distinct. Krieger, however, by finding and describing the real aecidium form of *Phragmidium Rubi* has cleared up this difficulty. It seems from the references to be found that Trelease first called the fungus *Caeoma nitens,* and that Curtis is responsible for *Uredo nitens* and ·*Uredo luminata.* The above terminalogy not being sufficient for the botanists of to-day, various combinations have been made and Schweinitz has been burdened as the authority in most cases. Such are *Uredo luminata, Caeoma* (*Uredo*) *luminatum, Uredo (Caeoma) nitens, Uredo caeoma-nitens, Caeoma nitens, Caeoma luminatum, Uredo luminatum, Uredo nitens, Aecidium luminatum.*

The history of the mature stage is briefer, perhaps on account of its late discovery. In 1869 Howe described a new Puccinia found on the raspberry as *P. Peckiana;* while the next year, Peck, finding it on the blackberry, and thinking it different, described it as *P. tripustulata.* Burrill, in 1885, called attention to these as identical, adding that they were now so considered by Peck. Lately, Tranzschel, by culture experiments connecting the Caeoma and the Puccinia, has taken the first specific name given to the Aecidium form and called the fungus *Puccinia interstitiale* (Schlechd). We believe, however, with Farlow,* and and it seems to be the usual method, that when such forms are found to be connected the specific name of the mature stage should be retained, in which case *Puccinia Peckiana,* Howe, is still proper and should be retained.

DISTRIBUTION.

From notes printed in various publications, the following distribution of the fungus has been obtained.

The aecidium stage has been reported as follows in the United States—Carolina, Schweinitz; Connecticut, Thaxter; Georgia, Ravenel; Illinois, Burrill; Iowa, Arthur; Kansas, Kellerman; Maryland, Brunk; Massachusetts, Sprague; Minnesota, Sheldon; Mississippi, Earle; Missouri, Demetrio; Nebraska, Webber; New Hampshire, Seymour; New Jersey, Britton; New York, Peck; Ohio, Detmers; Pennsylvania, Schweinitz; Texas, Jennings; West Virginia, Millspaugh; Wisconsin, Trelease. In Canada—Ottawa, Ellis & Everhart. In Europe—Bavaria,

---

*Proceedings American Academy of Arts and Sciences, 1883, p. 66.

Allescher; Finland, Kihlman; France, Cornu; Scandinavia, Eriksson; Russia, Tranzschel. In Asia—Siberia, Thümen; Kamtchatka, Schlechtendal. In European and Asiatic Russia, Tranzschel also gives the following: Gouv. St. Petersburg, Gouv. Archangelsk, Gouv. Moscow, Gouv. Esthland, N. Ural, and Minussinsk, and region of · Semipalatinska, and Enisseisk.

The stations of the teleutostage are more limited and as follows: In the United States—Illinois, Burrill; New York, Howe; Massachusetts, Farlow; Missouri, Galloway. In Europe—Lapland, Lagerheim; Russia, Tranzschel.

HOSTS.

The hosts of the aecidum stage are as follows: In the United States—*Rubus Canadensis, R. hispidus, R. occidentalis, R. strigosus, R. triflorus, R. trivialis, R. villosus.* In Europe and Asia—*R. saxatilis, R. arcticus.*

For the teleutostage hosts have been reported as follows: United States—*Rubus occidentalis, R. strigosus, R. villossus.* Europe—*R. arcticus, R. saxatilis.*

INDIVIDUAL HOSTS.

The following table proves an intimate relationship existing between this Caeoma and the Puccinia, as shown by their occupancy of the same individual plants.

INDIVIDUAL HOSTS OF CAEOMA AND PUCCINIA.

Spermagonia, May 17th.	Caeoma, June 9th.	Puccinia, July 6th-14th.
1. Raspberry. Leaves of old and new shoots affected.	Affected.	Old with few lower leaves still present and badly affected.
2. Rasp. Old and new affected.	Old affected.	Old nearly all dead, like lower, new badly affect'd.
3. Rasp. Old affected, new shoots not yet developed.	Old affected.	Dead, but some dead leaves slightly affected.
4. Rasp. Old and quite young new affected.	Old affected.	Dead, and leaves all dried up.
5. Rasp. Old free. The single new affected.	Old free. New affected.	Failed to find plant.
6. Rasp. No old. The single new partly affect'd	One new affected.	One lower leaf affected, near Caeoma affected leaf.
7. Rasp. Three old free. Two new affected	Two old free. Two new affected.	One old, lower leaves badly affected; single new affected live leaf.
8. Rasp. Old free. New affected.	Old free. Four new affected.	Old, nearly dead, slightly affected.
9. Rasp. One old free. Three new affected.	One old free. Three new affected.	Several new, nearly dead, free. One old affected.
10. Rasp. Three old free. Many small new mostly affected.	Three old, three new, free. Four new affected.	Old and new affected, some badly.

INDIVIDUAL HOSTS OF CÆOMA AND PUCCINIA—*Continued.*

Spermagonia, May 17th.	Caeoma, June 9th.	Puccinia, July 6th–14th.
11. Rasp. One old free. Five new affected.	One old free. Three new affected.	Several new, without lower leaves, free. One old, one new, affected.
12. Rasp. One old free. Bunch of new affected.	Two old, one new, free. Two new affected.	Old and new affected.
13. Rasp. One old free. One new affected.	One old free. One new affected.	Two new, with few lower leaves, free. One old affected.
14. Rasp. One old, one new affected.	One old affected.	Dead, but plant near badly affected.
15. Rasp. One new affected.	Failed to find plant.	Three new, lower leaves affected.
16. Rasp. Two old, some new, slightly affected.	Two old, two new, affected.	Two old, nearly dead, slightly affected; new, lower leaves slightly affected.
17. Rasp. One new affected.	One new affected.	One new, lower leaves mostly dead; but with one affected.
18. Rasp. One old free. Several new affected.	One old free. Two new affected,	Failed to find plant.
19. Rasp. Several old free. Several small new slightly affected.	One old, five new, free. Two new slightly affected.	A few lower leaves affected.
20. Rasp. One weak old free. Bunch of new affected.	Practically dead.	Practically dead, but with single live leaf affected.
21. Rasp. Bunch of new affected.	One new affected.	Slightly affected.
22. Rasp. One old, several new, affected.	One old free. One old, three new, affected.	Affected.
23. Rasp. Two old, one new, affected.	One new free. One old, one new, affected.	One new, with lower leaves affected.
24. Rasp. One old, nearly dead; several new, affected.	One old, five new, affected.	Practically dead, with two or three affected leaves.
25. Rasp. Several old affected. No new of importance.	Failed to find plant.	Dead.
26. Rasp. Two old free. Three new affected.	One old free. Three new affected.	One old, two new, affected.
27. Rasp. One old nearly dead, some new, affected.	Abundantly affected.	Practically dead, free.
28. Blackberry. Old nearly dead, some new, affected.	Abundantly affected.	Lower leaves affected.
29. Blackberry. One old nearly dead, some new, affected.	Abundantly affected.	Practically dead, some lower leaves affected.

INDIVIDUAL HOSTS OF CAEOMA AND PUCCINIA—*Continued.*

Spermagonia, May 17th.	Caeoma, June 9th.	Puccinia, July 6th-14th.
30. Rasp. Old nearly dead, some new, affect'd.	Affected.	Old without leaves; new without lower leaves; upper free.
31. Rasp. One old free. One new affected.	Abundantly affected.	A few lower leaves slightly affected.
32. Rasp. Two old free. One old, some new, affected.	Abundantly affected.	Failed to find plant.
33. Rasp. Two old, some new, affected.	Abundantly affected.	Old without leaves; new free.
34. Rasp. Old free. New, affected.	Abundantly affected.	Old affected; new, without lower leaves, free.

A number of the above plants were affected by the spermagonia and the aecidium stage on the new shoots only. This does not necessarily mean that those plants were affected for the first time, for the fungus may have had such a disastrous effect on those shoots infected the previous year as to have killed all of them, a thing quite apt to occur. It will also be seen that a number of plants were killed entirely. Of the living plants there were only three found in June that were not affected with the Puccinia, and these had their leaves so destroyed by the aecidium stage as to render subsequent infection unlikely.

The following serves as a sort of check to the above. These plants were examined at the same time as the above for the Puccinia. They were in the same locality, and at varying distances from plants affected by the aecidium stage; but, as none had been affected by this stage, their chance of being host to the Puccinia depended considerably on their distance from plants having the Caeoma. There were thirteen plants free and seven on which the Puccinia was found. All the affected ones were near plants that had the aecidium form.

a. Raspberry. A healthy plant. Two old, two new shoots, free. Several rods from plants affected with aecidium stage.
b. Rasp. Rather vigorous. One old, two new, free. Near a.
c. Rasp. Vigorous. Single new, apparently free. Near a.
d. Rasp. Sickly. One dead old, one new, free. Near a.
e. Rasp. Healthy. One old, two new, free. Two or three rods from affected plants.
f. Rasp. Rather sickly. Free. Near e.
g. Rasp. Rather sickly. One dead old, one new, free. Near e.
h. Rasp. One new free. One old with single leaf slightly affected. Three feet from affected plant 27.
i. Blackberry. Healthy. One old, one new, free. Five feet from affected plant 27.
j. Rasp. Vigorous. One old, one new, free. Three feet from affected plant 27.
k. Rasp. Two new free. One old, one new, rather abundantly affected. Two feet from affected plants 22, 23, 24, 25.
l. Rasp. One new free. One old affected. Near k.
m. Rasp. One old, one new, free. One old slightly affected. Near k.
n. Rasp. One old, several new, affected abundantly on lower leaves. Near k.
o. Rasp. One old, two new, rather abundantly affected. Near k.
p. Rasp. Several old and new free. Ten feet from two affected plants.

q. Rasp. Two old, two new, free. Near p.
r. Rasp. One old, one new, free. Near p.
s. Rasp. One old, one new, free. Close to an affected plant.
t. Rasp. Old and new affected. Close to affected plant.

*

Exsiccati.

In exsiccati the Caeoma and Puccinia here considered, on the dates given, were distributed under different names as follows:

1852, *Aecidium luminatum*, Schw., Ravenel's Fungi Caroliniani, V. 1, n. 91.

1876, *Uredo luminatum*, Curtis, on *Rubus Canadensis*, De Thümen's Mycotheca Universalis, C. V., n. 446.

1879, *Uredo luminatum*, (Schw.), on Rubus, Ravenel's Fungi Americani, C. III, n. 276.

1879, *Caeoma luminatum*, (Schw.), on *Rubus Strigosus*, Ellis' N. A. F., C. III, n. 277.

1885, *Caeoma nitens*, (S.), on *Rubus villosus, R. saxatilis*, Rabenhorst's Fungi Europaei, C. XXXIII, n. 3225, a. b. c.

*1887, *Caeoma nitens*, (Schw.), Eriksson's Fungi parasitici scandinavici, exsiccati, F. IV.

*1889, *Caeoma nitens*, Schw., on *Rubus villosus*, Kell. & Swingle's Kans. Fungi, F. II, n. 31.

*1890, *Caeoma nitens*, Schwein, on *Rubus saxatilis*, Allescher & Schnabl's Fungi Bavarici exsiccati, C. I.

1890, *Caeoma nitens*, (S.), on *Rubus Canadensis, R. villosus*, Seymour & Earle's Eco. Fungi, F. I., n. 27, 28.

1879, *Puccinia Peckiana*, Howe, on *Rubus occidentalis*, Ellis' N. A. F., C. III, n. 261.

1890, *Puccinia Peckiana*, Howe, on *Rubus villosus*, Seymour & Earle's Eco. Fungi, F. I., n. 26.

Literature.

The following references are such as have been used in the preparation of this paper. Scattered through agricultural and horticultural papers are notes on the "Orange Rust," which we have not cited, save in one or two instances. While it has been the intention to include all articles or notes of scientific importance on this subject, it is quite probable that some may have escaped observation.

Allescher, 1888, Bot. Centralblatt, B. XXXVI, p. 287, notes finding Caeoma nitens on Rubus saxatilis near Allach in 1878, and mistaking it for a form of Phragmidium Rubi.

Arthur, 1884, Bull. Iowa Agr. Coll., p. 164, lists C. nitens as occurring on blackberry in that state.

Bessey, 1885, Rep. Amer. Pom. Soc., p. 43, lists C. luminatum among the injurious fungi of horticulturists.

Botanisches Centralblatt, 1887, B. XXIX, p. 158, gives C. nitens as one of the fungi in the IV Fas. Fungi parasitici scandinavici, which appeared about this date.

Brendel, 1887, Flora Peoriana, p. 69, lists C. nitens from Peoria Co., Ill.

Britton, 1889, Geol. Surv. New Jersey, V. II, P. I. p. 503, gives Uredo luminata on R. strigosus from New Jersey.

Brunk, 1890, Ann. Rep. Md. Agr. Coll. and Ex. Sta., p. 115, mentions twenty varieties of blackberries affected by C. nitens, and gives notes on degree of affection. 1891 Rep. same publication, pp. 389 & 416, gives results of spraying and notes on varieties affected.

Burrill, 1882, Agr. Review, p. 88, gives an account of Caeoma luminatum. 1885, Parasitic Fungi of Illinois, P. I, pp. 178, 220, gives scientific descriptions of C. nitens and P. Peckiana, and suggests relationship. 1885, Rep. Ill. Industrial Univ., p. 115, writes scientific description of P.

Peckiana, also p. 138 same, of C. nitens, and suggests a connection between them.

1885, Prairie Farmer, V. LVII. p. 762, gives detailed structure of C. nitens, etc.

1885, Reprint from Amer. Soc. Micr., pp. 3, 8, gives general description and possible connections of C. nitens.

*Cobb, 1887, List Pl. Amherst, p. 39, gives Uredo luminata.

Cooke, 1878, Grevillea, V. VII, p. 46, lists Uredo luminatum from Georgia.

Cornu, 1881, Bull. Soc. Bot. France, p. 145, gives an account of finding Ae. luminatum on Rubus in France, mentioning it as new to Europe.

Cragin, 1885, Bull. Washburn Coll., V. I, n. 2, p. 68, lists C. luminatum from Kansas.

*Curtis, 1867, Bot. N. Car., p. 122, gives Uredo luminata.

Day, 1883, Cat. Plants of Buffalo and vicinity, gives Uredo luminata in the list.

Detmers, 1891, Ohio Ex. Sta., Bull. No. 6, p. 127, makes a general description of C. nitens with its effect on host.

1892, Same Pub., V. V, No. 7, p. 137, mentions finding what seems to be an uredo stage of C. nitens, etc.

1893, Same Pub., Tech. Series, V. I, No. 3, p. 180, describes further this supposed uredo form of Uredo (Caeoma) nitens, etc.

De Toni, 1888, Saccardo's Sylloge Fungorum, V. VII., P. II, p. 866, gives synonyms, hosts, and description of Uredo (Caeoma) nitens, also p. 699 treats P. Peckiana similarly.

Dietel, 1887, Botanisches Centralblatt, B. XXXII, p. 87, makes mere reference of variability of spores of P. Peckiana, as shown by Lagerheim, 1887.

1892, Bot. Centralblatt, B, XLIX, p. 270, gives reference to two articles on Russian Uredineae by Gobi and Tranzschel.

*Dietrich, 1859, Blicke in die Cryptogamenwelt der Ostseeprovinzen, abth. II, p. 492, describes, according to Tranzschel, this Caeoma as a new species, Uredo lucida.

Earle, 1889, U. S. Dept. Agr., Sec. Veg. Pathol., Bull. No. XI., pp 84, 85, 88, gives results of spraying with Bordeaux mixture blackberries affected with C. nitens.

*Ellis, 1889, Cat. Pl. New Jersey, 503, gives Uredo luminata.

Ellis & Everhart, 1885, Journal of Mycology, V. I, p. 86, give C. luminatum on R. triflorus from Ottawa, Canada.

Ex. Sta. Record, Vol. II, pp. 32, 455, 482; V. III, pp. 161, 313, 411, 722, makes reference to different Ex. Sta. notes on C. nitens.

Evans, 1893, Handbook Ex. Sta. Work, U. S. Dept. Agr., p. 283, gives account of general appearance of C. nitens.

Farlow, 1876, Bull. Bussey Institution, p. 432, lists P. Peckiana as occurring in Massachusetts.

1883, Proc. Amer. Academy Arts and Sciences, p. 76, gives a general description of appearance of Ae. nitens, and suggests that this may prove to be a heteroecious fungus.

Farlow & Seymour, 1888, Host Index U. S. Fungi, p. 37, give hosts and synonyms of C. nitens and P. Peckiana.

*Frost, 1875, Cat. Pl. Amherst, p. 84, lists Uredo luminata.

Galloway, 1889, U. S. Dept. Agr., Bot. Div., Bull. VIII, pp. 56, 58, lists C. nitens and P. Peckiana from Missouri.

1889, Rep. U. S. Dept. Agr., p. 416, speaks of spraying experiments made by Earle. Printed in 1890.

Gardner's Monthly, 1871, pp. 211, 266, correspondents give notes on "orange rust" of blackberry, treatment, etc.

Hoffman, 1863, Index Fungorum, p. 3, lists Ae. luminatum with "nitens" as the synonym.

Howe, 1869, (23) Rep. Bot. N. Y. State Museum, p. 57, gives description of a new fungus, Puccinia Peckiana, on Rubus occidentalis. Printed in 1872.

Humphrey, 1890, Ann. Rep. Mass. Ex. Sta., p. 224, mentions C. nitens as common there, etc. Printed in 1891.

Jennings, 1890, Texas Ex. Sta., Bull. No. IX, p. 23, mentions C. nitens as quite a drawback to culture of blackberry, and mentions it as also found on wild plants of R. trivialis.

Journal of Mycology, 1889, p. 103, gives reference to Lagerheim's 1889 article and p. 161, lists C. nitens as in Kellermann & Swingle's Kans. Fungi, Fas. II.

Kellerman, 1885, Washburn Coll. Bull., V. I, n. 2, p. 74, gives host of C. nitens in Kansas.

Karsten, 1879, Mycologia Fennica, P. IV, p. 51, describes what is probably C. nitens as aecidium form of Phragmidium bulbosum (Ph. Rubi).

Lagerheim, 1887, Botanisker Notiser, p. 60, gives an account of finding P. Peckiana on R. arcticus in Lapland, discusses forms of this fungus as found in different localities, and suggests C. nitens as a stage of Ph. Rubi rather than of P. Peckiana.

1889, Hedwigia, B. XXVIII, H. 2, p. 110, treats of distribution, of hosts, and of the relationship of C. nitens to other forms, and, as Krieger has found the aecidium stage of Ph. Rubi, now thinks the Caeoma heteroecious.

1890, Hedwigia, p. 173, gives mere reference to variability of position of germ pore of P. Peckiana.

Link, 1825, Species Plantorum, T. VI, P. II, p. 61, n. 166, describes C. luminatum and gives its host and locality as taken from Schweinitz, but instead of adopting the latter's name for the fungus gives it one on his own account.

Same, p. 32, n. 89, gives description, hosts, locality and name of Schlechtendal's (1820) Caeoma interstitiale,

Ludwig, 1884, Bot. Cent., B. XX, p. 356, reviews Trelease's 1884 article.

1887, Botanisches Centralblatt, B. XXXI, p. 162, makes a short abstract of Lagerheim's 1887 article.

Magnus, 1890, Separat-Abdruck aus Hedwigia, H. 6, gives C. nitens as one of the interesting fungi in Cent. I, Fungi Bavarici.

Millspaugh, 1892, West Va. Agr. Ex. Sta. Bull., n. 24, p. 509, gives C. nitens as found in that state on R. hispidus.

Newcombe, 1891, Jour. Mycology, Vol. IV. p. 106, proves mycelium of C. nitens to be perennial in its host. Remarks by Galloway on consequent treatment.

New York Agr. Ex. Sta., Bull. n. 36, p. 641, mentions orange rust as a troublesome disease of raspberry.

Oudemans, 1891, Hedwigia, H. 3, p. 178, refers to Caeoma interstitiale published by Schlechtendal in 1820, it being collected by Ehrenberg in 1817 in Kamtchatka on Rubus arcticus, states that the illustration given of this fungus corresponds exactly with that of C. nitens, which must now be known as C. interstitiale, as this one was published two years earlier.

Peck, 1868, (22nd) Rep. Bot. N. Y. State Museum, p. 92, lists Uredo luminata as common on Rubus. Printed in 1869.

1870, (24th) Rep. p. 91, gives scientific description of Puccinia tripustulata, n. s. found on Rubus villosus. Printed in 1872.

1871, (25th) Rep. pp. 113, 114, gives scientific descriptions of P. tripustulata, Pk. and P. Peckiana, Howe, which at that time he considered distinct. Printed in 1873.

1873, (27th) Rep. p. 77, notes Uredo luminata as rapidly becoming a serious drawback to the culture of blackberries and raspberries. Printed in 1875.

1875, (29th) Rep. p. 72, lists P. Peckiana and P. tripustulata, also p. 75, lists Uredo luminata as found there on R. villosus, R. Canadensis, R. occidentalis, R. strigosus. Printed in 1878.

Richards, 1893, Proc. Amer. Acad. Arts and Sciences, p. 31, treats of development of the spermagonia of C. nitens, and states that they do not originate in one greatly enlarged epidermal cell.

*Schlechtendal, 1820, Horae physicae Berolinenses, p. 96, t. 20, f. 13., describes and figures C. interstitiale as new, it being collected by Ehrenberg in Kamtchatka in 1817 on R. arcticus.

Schroeter, Ein Beitrag zur Kenntniss der nordischen Pilze. p. 7, gives C. nitens as found in Sweden.

Schweinitz, 1822, Synop. Fungi Carolina, p. 69, n. 458, describes Ae. nitens, n. s. on Rubus strigosus.

    1831, North Amer. Fungi, p. 293, n. 2887, gives his former Ae. nitens as Caeoma (Aecidium) luminatum, Schw., his specimen this time being from Pennsylvania. Printed, 1834.

Scribner, 1886, Rep. U. S. Dept. Agr., p. 133, lists C. nitens from Michigan. Printed 1887.

Seymour, 1886, Reprint from Minn. Hort. Rep., V. XIV, gives some facts concerning life history of C. nitens.

    1887 Amer. Naturalist, p. 1115, notes a more erect and rigid growth of plants attacked by C. nitens.

Sprague, 1856, Proc. Boston Nat. Hist. Soc., p. 328, lists Uredo nitens as occurring in Massachusetts.

Sprengel, 1827, L. Sys. Veg. 16 ed., V. IV, p. 574, gives scientific description of Uredo interstitialis, Schl., which he considers the same as Aecidium nitens, Schw.

Streinz, 1862, Nomenclator fungorum, p. 644, n. 10757, gives Uredo interstitialis, Spr., with Ae. nitens, Schw., C. interstitiale, Lk., and C. luminatum, Lk. as synonyms.

Thaxter, 1889, Ann. Rep. Conn. Ex. Sta., p. 172, gives C. nitens as common on cultivated and wild raspberries and blackberries, and suggests method of treatment. Printed in 1890.

*Thümen, 1880, Beitrage zur Pilz-Flora Sibiriens, III, p. 14 gives Uredo luminata as found in Asiatic Siberia.

Tranzschel, 1892, St. Petersburg Naturforscher Gesellschaft (Bot. Section), gives preliminary report on producing P. Peckiana by means of artificial infection of R. saxatilis with spores of C. interstitiale (C. nitens).

    1893, Hedwigia, H. V., p. 257, gives further successful results of artificial infection, and concludes that the Caeoma and the Puccinia must hereafter be known as stages of Puccinia interstitiale (Schl.)

Trelease, 1884, Extract from Trans. Wis. Academy of Science, Arts and Letters, V. VI, p. 30 gives host of C. nitens in Wisconsin. ! Probably the first to call this fungus Caeoma nitens.

    1884. Psyche, V. IV, p. 195, notes insect larvae as eating spores of C. nitens.

Underwood & Cook, 1889, Illustr. Fungi, 51, give C. nitens.

Watt, 1885, Canadian Naturalist and Geologist, Second Series, V. II, p. 391, gives Ae. laminatum, the specific term probably being "luminatum" misspelled.

Webber, 1889, Extract from Rep. Neb. State Board of Agr., p. 73, notes Uredo (C.) nitens as being very destructive.

    1889, Neb. Agr. Ex. Sta., Bull. No. 11, lists same on p. 65, and Pond mentions it on p. 89.

Winter, 1884, Rabenhorst's Kryptogamen Flora I-I, p. 230, gives Karsten's (1879) description of I stage of Ph. Rubi, although he states that he has never seen the same for certain.

    1885, Hedwigia, B. XXIV, p. 181, gives C. nitens on R. villosus and R. Canadensis, as sent from Missouri by Demetrio.

    1885, Rabenhorst's Fungi Europaei, C. XXXIII, n. 3225, presents specimens of C. nitens for America and Fennia, and says that Fennia specimens are C. nitens rather than a form of Ph. Rubi for which they were sent to him.

G. P. CLINTON, B.S., Assistant Botanist.

EXPLANATION OF PLATES.

- Plate 1.   Fig. 1.   Under surface of blackberry leaf thickly covered with sori of aecidium stage.

      Fig. 2.   Under surface of raspberry leaflet, with both aecidio- and teleuto-sori.

      Fig. 3.   Under surface of blackberry leaflet, with teleutosori in groups.

      Fig. 4.   Upper surface of raspberry leaflet, with peculiar mottled appearance frequently caused by teleutostage of fungus.

      Fig. 5.   Cross section of blackberry leaflet through a sorus of the aecidium stage.

Plate 2.   Fig 1.   Cross section showing part of blackberry leaflet with a spermagonium beginning to form just beneath the epidermis.

      Fig. 2.   Slightly more advanced stage.

      Fig. 3.   Mature spermagonium in cross section.

Plate 3.   Fig. 1-4.   Haustoria in pith of very young shoot of blackberry, as seen in cross section. 2 and 3 show the peculiar conjugation sometimes found.

      Fig. 5-7.   Haustoria in pith of old blackberry stems, in cross section, 5 and 6 being more highly magnified than 7.

      Fig. 8-9.   Mycelium in longitudinal sections of blackberry pith, 8 being from a young and 9 from an old cane.

      Fig 10.   Section with mycelium and a haustorium in parenchyma tissue of very young leaf.

      Fig. 11-13   Cross section of parenchyma cells in cortex of root, with mycelium of fungus, 11 showing cross end of mycleium between the cells, 12 and 13 haustoria.

      Fig. 14.   Tangential section with mycelium and a haustorium in parenchyma cells of root cortex.

Plate 4.   Fig. 1-21.   Aecidiospores germinating in water.

      Fig. 1-7.   Germination of same spore at end of 4, 5, 6, 7, 8, 9, and 24 hours.

      Fig. 8-12.   Germination of spores during first two days, and 13 during third day.

      Fig. 14-18.   Spores from raspberry, having been 48 hours in water, while 19-20 show quicker germination at end of 24 hours.

      Fig. 21.   Peculiar tips of germ tubes, two showing suddenly enlarged tips, and three flexuous tips.

      Fig. 22.   Aecidiospores that were placed on lower moist surface of blackberry leaf, showing contracted tip of germ tube, and method of entrance through stomates.

      Fig. 23.   Peculiar branch of germ tube of a spore sown on blackberry leaf.

      Fig. 24-29.   Teleutospores germinated in water, at end of eight days. 24, 26, 28, 29, optical sections of the spores, showing how germ tube penetrates the exospore.

      Fig. 30.   Mycelium as seen beneath epidermis, and between guard cells of stomates. From blackberry leaflet just beginning to show teleutoform.

PLATE I.

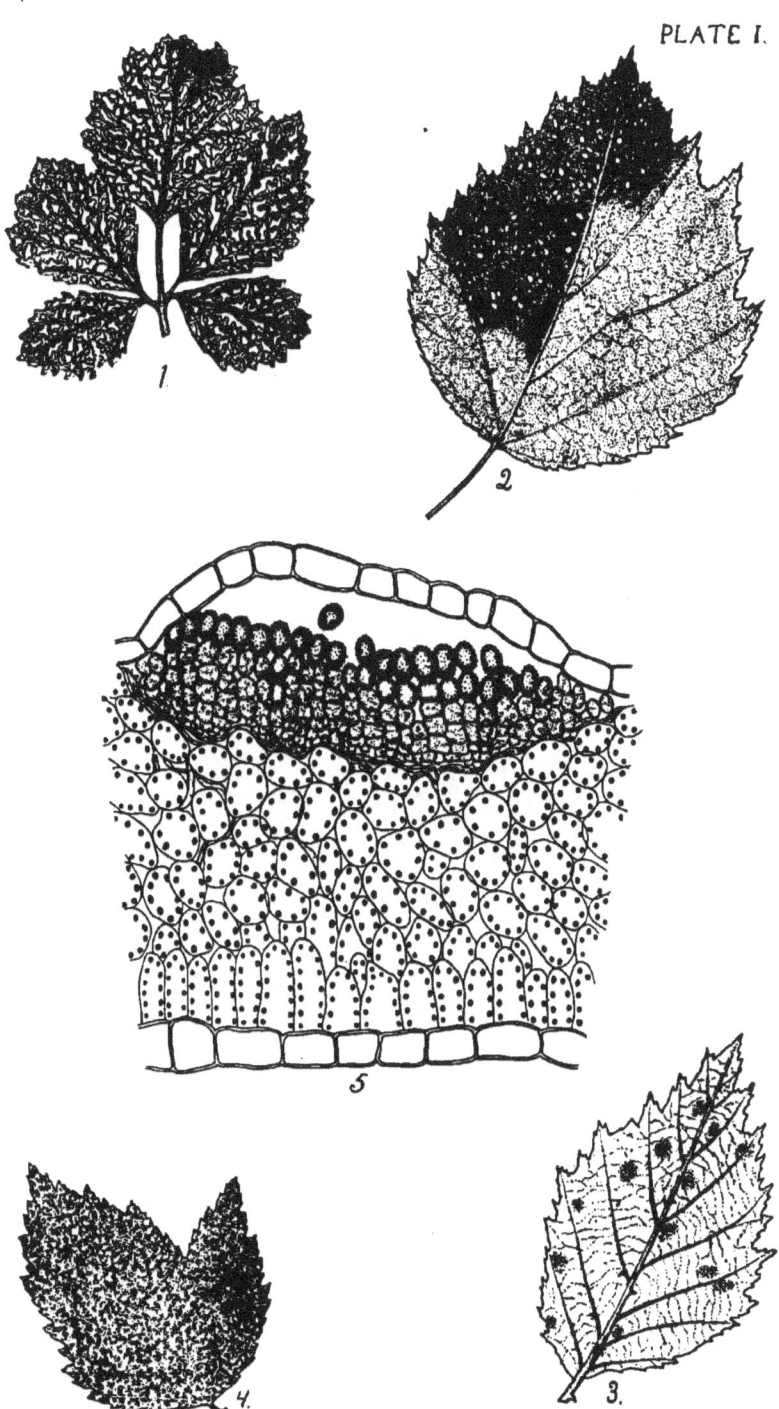

PLATE II.

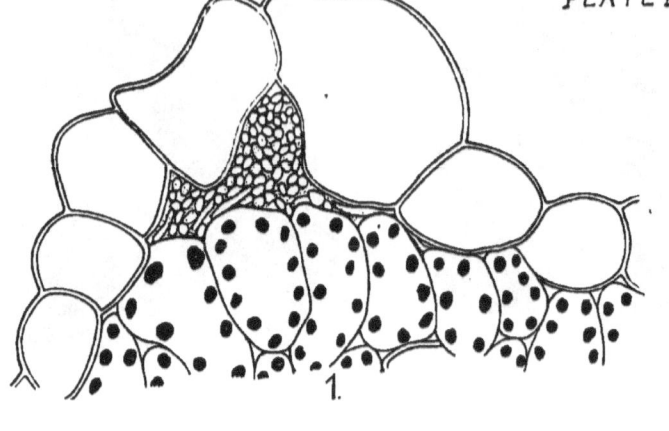

1.

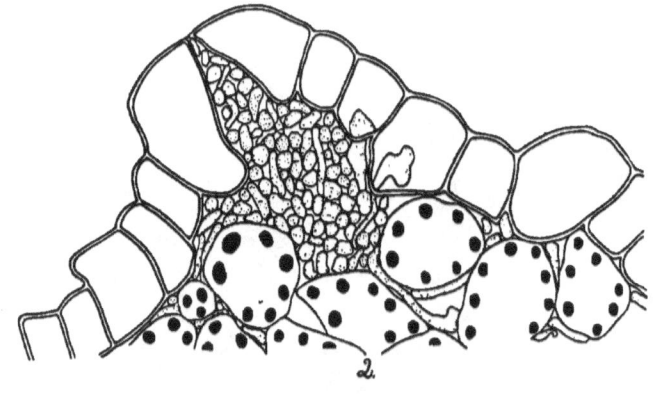

2.

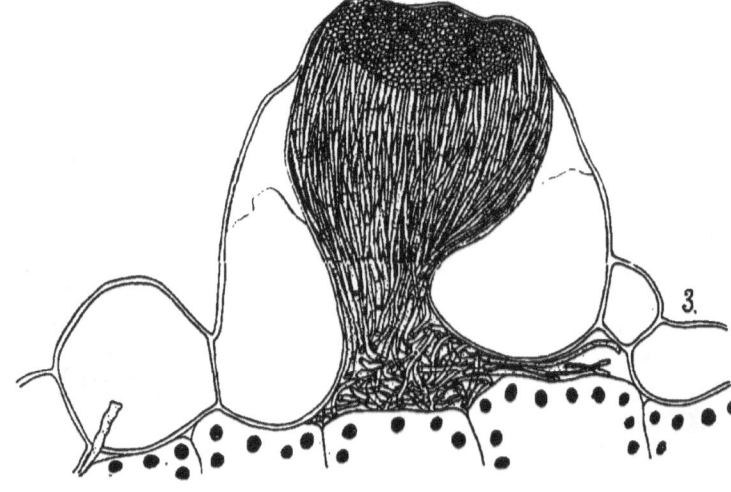

3.

PLATE III.

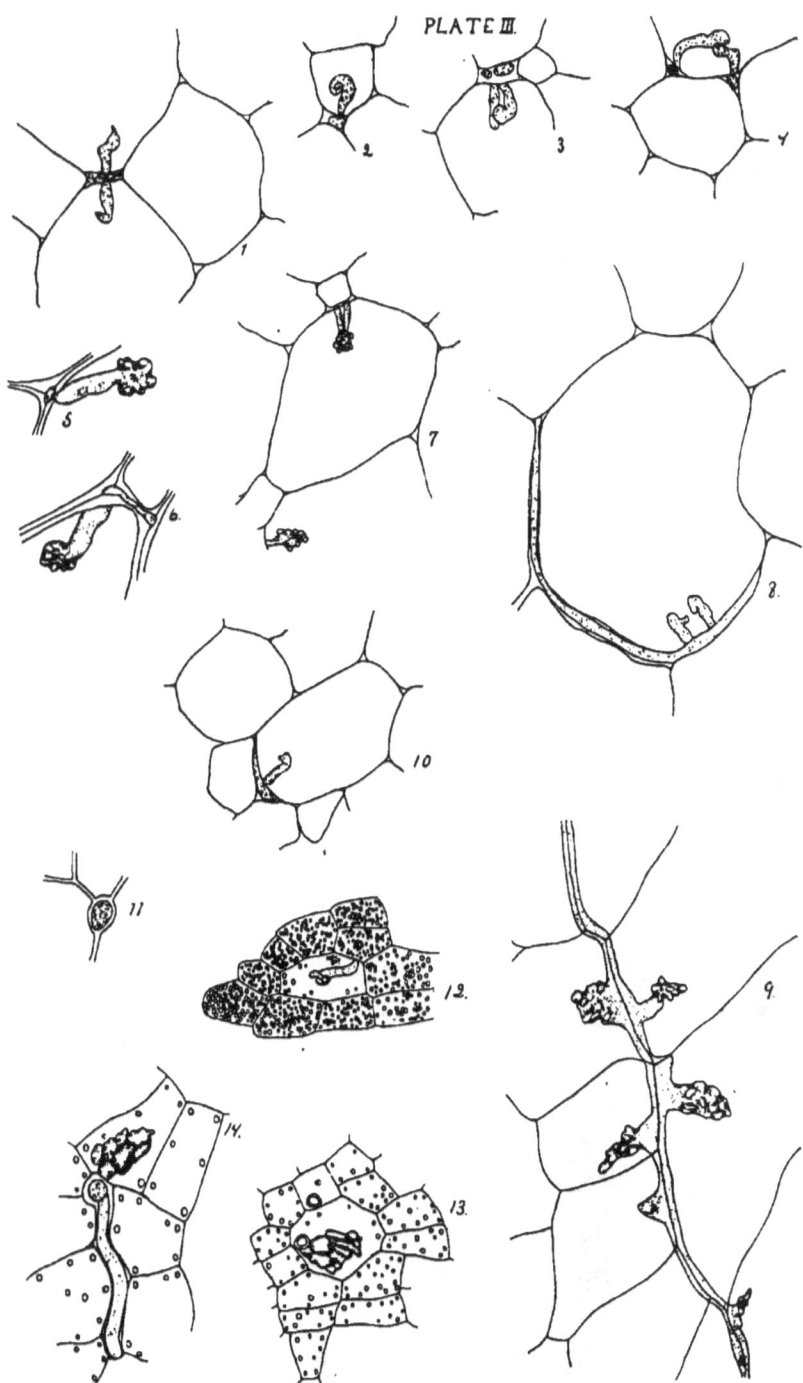

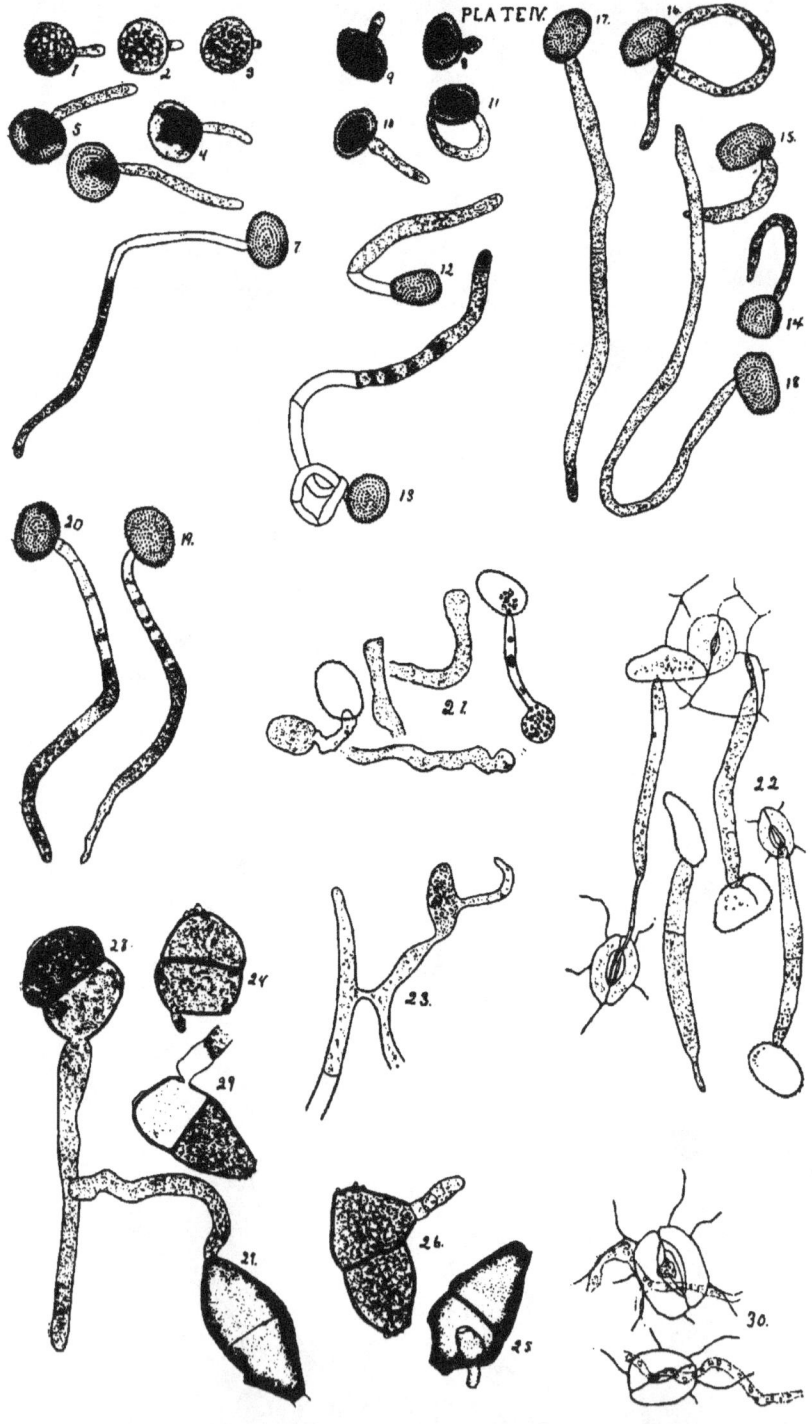

PLATE IV.

*A NEW FACTOR IN ECONOMIC AGRICULTURE.

Economic agriculture has in store many problems whose solution will greatly lessen labor while at the same time increasing the productiveness of the soil. There is no subject of greater interest and importance to physiological botany and agriculture than the recently discovered symbiotic relation between different organisms; a relation mutually beneficial and in many cases absolutely necessary to existence. It is the purpose of this paper to discuss a form of symbiosis which may prove to be of special interest to agriculture. Taking it for granted that most readers of these bulletins are practically unacquainted with the subject " Symbiosis," a condensed historical review of it from its beginning will be first given.

[*It has been well known for many years that clover, especially when plowed under, made a very marked contribution to the fertility of the soil upon which it grew, and later scientific investigations have shown that this plant, and some other allied ones, have the peculiarity of making use of the free nitrogen of the air as an element in their nutrition. Most other plants cannot do this, though all must have nitrogen as a food ingredient. It is usually taken from the soil in combination with other elements; as, for instance, in the lime forming nitrate of lime. Now four-fifths of the atmosphere is free nitrogen. If by any means plants can make use of it as food, they have an abundant and constant supply at hand and the combined form in the soil then becomes less important, or unnecessary. Since the latter is the most expensive of artificial fertilizers and its application is often demanded for full crops, any substitute for it must be of immense practical value.

It has now been shown that clover, like other agricultural plants, is of itself incapable of utilizing free nitrogen, but that it does so through the agency of low organisms (bacteria) found in little knots or tubercles which form like galls upon the roots. Such tubercles are found on the roots of all plants which are known to gain nutrition from free nitrogen and are not so found upon any other plants. They are not found upon the roots of any of the grasses or cereals. Can the organisms be made to grow upon these roots by any artificial means?

It must be confessed that it would have been exceedingly hazardous for any one to have expressed an affirmative opinion upon this question; but the vast importance of the matter made it desirable to try anything which gave the least promise of success. In this condition of things it came to the knowledge of officers of this Experiment Station that Dr. Albert Schneider, then of Minneapolis, Minn., had found from some preliminary investigations indications of the possibility of adapting the organisms by artificial cultivation to growth upon the roots of maize or of other cereals. He was therefore secured to continue these investigations during the latter part of the summer of 1893, and was given all the facilities at the command of the Station. The following from his pen gives the results as far as obtained. While little direct evidence has been gained in favor of ultimate success, it is considered desirable to publish an account of the work so far done with the hope of being able at some future time to add greatly to the information now obtained. The report is necessarily technical in form and several terms are employed that may be new to many who read these pages; but the subject matter is also new to the public and other wording could scarcely make it easier to comprehend. The term *symbiosis* is applied to the association of two different kinds of living plants or animals in a mutually helpful relation.

THOMAS J. BURRILL, Horticulturist and Botanist.]

301

BRIEF HISTORICAL REVIEW.

The term symbiosis was first used by de Bary in 1879 in an article entitled, *Die Erscheinung der Symbiose.* By it he meant that kind of commensalism or consortism between different organisms which proved mutually beneficial. In parasitism the benefit is always one-sided, one organism flourishing at the expense of the other. The most familiar form of symbiosis is to be found in the case of lichens. Here we find an ordinary hyphal fungus living in vital relation with a filamentous or single-celled alga. The chlorophyll bearing algae make it possible for the fungus to develop on rocks and tree trunks where it could not exist alone. In turn the alga absorbs nourishment from the fungus. It is only a few years since the algae of lichens were looked upon as spores and hence named gonidia. The dual nature of lichens has been demonstrated both by analysis and synthesis. The algal and fungal portions of a given lichen have been separated and each found to be capable of existing alone. It has been found that by placing a certain fungus and alga together they form a true lichen.

A form of symbiosis of much greater importance is to be found with certain forest trees. Often the greater portion of nourishment is supplied by fungi. These fungi stand in symbiotic relation with the small rootlets of the tree forming a structure part root and part fungus, called a Mycorhiza. According to the researches of Frank the significance of this root symbiosis is to be explained as follows: The tree as well as the fungus requires humus; but the humus, before it can be readily taken up as food by the trees, must first be assimilated by the fungus. Frank and his pupil Schlicht have found symbiotic fungi among Ericaceae, Epadridiae, Empetraceae, and Orchidaceae.

Among the Leguminosae we meet still another form of symbiosis. Here one of the symbionts is a bacterium (Rhizobium) and is always to be found within the tissue of the host forming swellings called tubercles. The history of Rhizobia tubercles is very interesting and has led to many controversies.

The tubercles on the roots of Leguminosae had been noted as early as 1852, though no one understood their meaning. Malpighi considered them as galls; de Condolle, as pathological growths. Clos looked upon them as lenticular growths, while Treviranus, considered them undeveloped buds. Eriksson gave a more complete description of the tubercles of *Faba vulgaris.* In 1866 Woronin noticed that the soft parenchymatous cells of the interior of the tubercles were entirely filled with small bodies. He pronounced these bacteria. Most botanists coincided with Woronin as to the bacterial nature of the tubercle contents. These bacteria were looked upon as true parasites. In 1879 Frank pointed out that it was not an ordinary form of parasitism. In 1887 Hellriegel concluded a series of experiments which led him to the conclusion that there was some close relation between the root tubercles of Leguminosae and

free nitrogen assimilation. Beginning with 1885 and ending in 1891, a
heated controversy was kept up concerning the contents of the infected
cells of tubercles. Heretofore they had been looked upon as bacteria.
Brunchorst and Tschirch conducted a series of experiments in Frank's
institute which led them to believe that the bacteria, so-called, were not
bacteria but were bacteroid bodies formed by the plants themselves;
that is, the bacteria-like particles were albuminous reserve products
which were finally absorbed by the plant and utilized in maturing the
seed. Frank readily seconded these conclusions. Brunchorst named
these bacteria-like albuminous substances *Bakteroiden*.

Eriksson had already noted in some tubercles peculiar hyphal
structures penetrating the tubercle. He asserts that these hyphae end
in the meristem of the tubercle and that the *Bakteroiden* bud off from
them within the vegetable cell. In 1887 Marshall Ward made a special
study of the mode of infection in *Vicia Faba.* His observations coincided quite closely with those of Eriksson. The above mentioned hyphal
structures Ward looked upon as true hyphae of a fungus belonging to
the Ustilagineae. The *Bakteroiden* he considered as the spores. According to Vuillemin the *Bakteroiden* are simply differentiations of the
cell protoplasm and the hyphal structures are to be looked upon as the
tubercle producing organism. He maintains that he succeeded in staining a cell membrane and hence called it a true hyphal fungus belonging
to the Chytridiaceae, naming it *Cladochytrium leguminosarum*. Beyerinck looked upon these hyphal structures as mere *Schleimfäden*, produced
by the plant cells themselves. He supposed them to be formed from
the remnants of spindle threads left after nuclear division had taken
place. Relying upon this assumption he also endeavored to explain the
fact that the *Schleimfäden* pass directly through the cell wall. The
Bakteroiden Beyerinck considered the infecting organisms, formed
from the microsomatic bodies found in the meristem cells of the tubercles. The microsomatic bodies were looked upon as bacteria which
normally live within the soil but which are enabled to enter the plant
root in some unknown way. He also seconded Brunchorst's and Frank's
conclusions that the *Bakteroiden* are re-absorbed by the plant. Prazmowski
looked upon the hyphal structure as a plasmodium filled with bacilli-
like organisms. As soon as these enter the root parenchyma the plasmodium surrounds the cell protoplasm so that cell protoplasm, plasmodium, and the bacilli-like bodies form a thorough mixture. Here the
bacilli-like bodies are converted into the *Bakteroiden*. Later Prazmowski
changes his opinion, maintaining that the plasmodium is a hyphae-like
tube filled with bacteria. The spores of the bacteria enter the root
hairs in some way and multiply enormously. The bacteria tube pushes
forward as far as the meristem of the tubercle where it dissolves and
liberates the bacteria; the latter become mixed with the cell protoplasm,
and are finally converted into the peculiar *Bakteroiden*. Schroeter considered the hyphal structures as true plasmodia of a fungus belonging to

the Myxomycetes.   This fungus he named *Phytomyxa leguminosarum*. Frank came to the conclusion that the hyphal structures were products of the plant cells themselves, and served the purpose of assisting the Rhizobia into the root parenchyma, hence he named them *Infektionsfäden*.

According to Frank infection takes place as follows: The roots of Leguminosae secrete a substance which serves as an attraction to the Rhizobia in the soil.   They accumulate and multiply on the surface of the root, some of them enter the outer cells and are then conducted into the interior by the *Infektionsfäden*.   Here the Rhizobium assimilates the cell protoplasm and becomes much changed in form, finally becoming converted into *Bakteroiden*.   In 1890 he believed with Brunchorst that the *Bakteroiden* were albuminoid bodies formed from the cell protoplasm, in which the Rhizobia were imbedded.   In 1891 he changes his opinion in regard to *Bakteroiden* maintaining that they are true bacteria, as stated above.

So far Frank adheres to the opinion that there is but one species of Rhizobium, namely: *Rhizobium leguminosarum*.   Investigations by the writer have led to the belief that there are at least several species. One and the same species may be found on different plants.   For example, one species, designated *Rhizobium curvum*, was noticed on *Phaseolus paucifloris;* another, *Rhizobium mutabile*, was found on *Trifolium pratense* and *Trifolium repens*, on *Melilotus alba* and *Medicago sativa*.   The much discussed *Infektionsfäden* seem to bear an incidental relation only to the Rhizobia.   It is not probable that the roots of Leguminosae secrete or excrete a substance that is attractive to Rhizobia.   All later experiments, as far as known, verify these statements.   Rhizobia in some way gain access to the surface cells of the roots and multiply and produce their peculiar changes in plant economy. Elsewhere the writer has described the root tubercle morphology and hence will not take up space here.   It should be said, however, that the root tubercles are quite permanent in structure; and that it does not seem to the writer that the contents of Rhizobia and tubercles are at any time directly reabsorbed by the plant.

It would be impossible to review all the work that has been done in regard to the root tubercles and the free nitrogen assimilating Rhizobia they contain.   Carefully considered and weighed, the discussions and controversies up to date may be summarized as follows:

1.   Certain bacteria, called Rhizobia, live in symbiotic or mutually beneficial relations with certain higher plants, especially the Leguminosae.

2.   Plants can develop without these Rhizobia, but, as a rule, thrive much better with them.

3.   These Rhizobia have the power of assimilating for the use of the plant the free nitrogen of the air.

4.   There are several species of Rhizobia.

5. *Rhizobium mutabile* very likely stands preëminent in the nitrogen assimilating function.

6. The *Infektionsfäden* probably have no essential relation to the Rhizobia.

7. The tubercles are abnormal growths produced by the presence of the Rhizobia.

8. The tubercles have a definite structure and form a permanent, coherent part of the root.

9. The *Bakteroiden* of Brunchorst (*Rhizobia mutabile*) are capable of being cultivated in suitable media.

PLAN OF RESEARCH.

The plan, though in a certain sense original, did not suggest itself spontaneously, but is the result of careful study.

That the Rhizobia play an important part in the vegetable kingdom is definitely settled. The results of Hellriegel's, Willfarth's, Lawes and Gilbert's, and Frank's experiments have opened a new era in economic agriculture. They have begun a work which will doubtless result in some great good.

Several interesting problems suggest themselves for solution. One, to which attention is here directed, is to ascertain if the Rhizobia of Leguminosae can be induced to live in symbiotic relation with plants of other families, as, for example, the Gramineae. If, for instance, the Rhizobium of the *Melilotus alba* root can be transplanted to the *Zea Mays* root and there continue its nitrogen-assimilating function, then our corn crop can be doubled and trebled with the same amount of labor now expended on an average crop. Of course it must be left for the future to decide whether this can be done. So far as known no experiments have as yet been attempted in this line. Knowledge of Rhizobia and bacteria in general leads to the belief that satisfactory results may be obtained. A brief outline of the plan of research which suggests itself is as follows:

1. To make a suitable culture medium.

2. To develop Rhizobia in this culture medium.

3. To change the culture medium by degrees from a leguminous nature to a gramineous nature.

4   To modify the Rhizobia by successively transferring from a highly leguminous medium to a highly gramineous medium.

5. To inoculate Gramineae with modified Rhizobia.

6. Life history of Rhizobia.

First, to make a suitable culture medium. Naturally, in order to induce the Rhizobia to develop outside of roots, there must be supplied artificially conditions approaching those of nature. Rhizobia, as they are found in root tubercles, are placed under the following conditions: 1. They are in a vegetable medium. 2. The medium is slightly acid in reaction. 3. They are not exposed to light. Artificially, these conditions can be supplied as follows: Instead of using the ordinary gelatine-peptone bouillon the purpose is to prepare a special culture medium from agar-agar and a water extract of certain leguminous roots, which is then made slightly acid in reaction and placed in the dark after being inoculated with a given species of Rhizobium. By this means all the above mentioned essential conditions are met with. Frank's (as well as those of others) failures to make cultures of the so called *Bakteroiden* were probably due to the fact that he did not supply the required conditions. Frank used gelatine-peptone bouillon. He neither mentions the reaction nor the light conditions. The writer attempted cultures in both gelatine-peptone and agar-agar bouillon, slightly alkaline in reaction and placed in the dark after being inoculated. *Bakteroiden* (*Rhizobium mutibile*) were not thus developed, but there was readily obtained a culture of *Rhizobiam Frankii*, var. *majus*. Recently Atkinson has succeeded in cultivating the *Bakteroiden* of vetch in an agar-agar peptone-vetch culture, which demonstrates conclusively that the *Bakteroiden* are true bacteria. The plan of the writer is to modify somewhat Atkinson's culture medium, and to omit the peptone which is an animal product. Instead of making an extract of the entire plant, roots only will be used. Atkinson does not state the reaction of his culture media, though it is to be supposed that they were acid, as vegetable cell sap is normally acid. Presumably he kept his cultures in diffused light, as he does not mention anything to the contrary. There would seem to be but little difficulty in preparing a suitable culture medium in which to develop Rhizobia.

The second step is, to develop Rhizobia in this special culture medium. The desire is to cultivate *Rhizobium mutabile* (*Bakteroiden* of Brunch.), as it is believed to be the one which has, preëminently, the power to assimilate free nitrogen. Since Atkinson has demonstrated that it can be cultivated, no doubts need be entertained on that score. All that is required is to place it in the proper medium under antiseptic precautions. Being once assured of a pure culture of *Rhizobium mutabile*, considerable progress is made toward the solution of the problem under consideration.

The third step, to change the culture medium by degrees from a leguminous nature to a gramineous nature, is of great importance. It is a well known fact that low organisms, especially bacteria, may become modified so as to adapt themselves to environments which proved fatal before they were thus modified. The purpose is to change the culture media so as to induce the Rhizobia to become modified. The plan is as follows: To make culture media in which the agar-agar is present in a constant percentage and the vegetable extracts variable. As already indicated the plan is to modify Rhizobia of a given leguminous plant so as to be capable of transplanting to the roots of a given gramineous plant. To begin with a culture medium will be taken which contains the fixed quantity of agar-agar and 100 per cent of extract of Melilotus roots; the culture medium next in the series shall contain 80 per cent Melilotus root extract and 20 per cent of *Zea Mays* root extract; the next in the series shall contain 60 per cent of Melilotus extract and 40 per cent of Zea extract and so on, each of the series differing by 20 per cent in the relative amounts of sweet clover and corn root extracts. At one end of the series is a culture containing 100 per cent of *Melilotus alba* root extract; at the other end, a culture containing 100 per cent *Zea Mays* root extract.

The fourth step explains itself from what has already been stated. The Rhizobia are to be transferred from one culture medium to another until they have passed through the series. By that time they are supposed to have become modified to such an extent as to grow and multiply in roots of corn.

This is to be attempted in the fifth step, to inoculate Gramineae with modified Rhizobia. The inoculation must be conducted with great care. Plants to be experimented upon should be placed in special glass jars. In place of soil, quartz sand will be used with culture solution. Plants must be grown in a medium which can be made perfectly sterile. The modified Rhizobia are to be transferred from the culture to the vessel containing the sterilized corn plants.

Lastly, the behavior of Rhizobia, will be carefully noted and their life history more carefully studied. Their behavior under normal and abnormal surroundings will be observed. Though present knowledge concerning the life history of Rhizobia warrants undertaking the experiments just outlined, yet it is quite essential that their life history should be more thoroughly studied, especially in regard to the following conditions:

1.   *Temperature.*—(*a*) Minimum.   (*b*) Optimum.   (*c*) Maximum.
2.   *Light.*—(*a*) Darkness.   (*b*) Semi-darkness.   (*c*) Green.   (*d*) Blue.   (*e*) Red. (*f*) Yellow.   (*g*) White light (diffused).   (*h*) White light (direct).
3.   *Moisture.*—(*a*) Very dry.   (*b*) Moderately moist.   (*c*) Very moist.
4.   *Atmospheric Pressure.*—(*a*) High pressure.   (*b*) Low pressure.
5.   *Heliotropism.*—
6.   *Hydrotropism.*—
7.   *Geotropism.*—

These experiments are not undertaken with any desire to magnify unduly the importance of bacteria, nor with absolute confidence of success. As already stated, the present knowledge of Rhizobia and bacteria in general justifies undertaking these experiments.

RESEARCH.

The first thing was to prepare suitable culture media in which to grow Rhizobia. For this purpose two aqueous extracts were made from *Melilotus alba*, one from the roots, rootlets, and tubercles; the other from the upper portions of stems and leaves. They were prepared in the following manner: About one-half a kilogram of roots and rootlets were weighed, carefully washed, then finely chopped, and put in a jar with one liter of distilled water. This was allowed to stand in a cool place for twenty-four hours, being shaken occasionally. The juice was then squeezed out through cloth into a beaker, and ten grams of agar were added. After standing for twelve hours the whole was heated to near the boiling point until the agar was dissolved. It was then filtered through coarse filter paper in a hot water filter. The agar extract medium of stems and leaves was prepared in a similar way. To portions of these filtered media were added peptonum, pancreatin, and salt in various proportions. Some neutral and slightly alkaline media were made by the addition of sodium carbonate solution. Litmus paper tests showed that the normal extracts of Melilotus roots and stems were acid in reaction, the latter more highly than the former. These various culture media were now ready for use.

Next, plants of *Melilotus alba* with normal, fully formed root tubercles were secured. The tubercles were removed, washed in distilled water, and quickly dried with blotting paper which had been passed through the flame of a Bunsen burner. The tubercle was then passed through the flame and cut with a sharp, sterilized knife, care being taken not to allow the knife blade to drag over the cut surface. Test tubes with culture media were then inoculated from the cut surface by means of a platinum needle. These inoculated test tubes, numbering about fifty, were set aside in a dark chamber at the normal summer temperature of the room. In about four or five days a whitish growth was noticed in most tubes containing agar extract of Melilotus roots. Examination under a medium power showed that they consisted of organisms resembling in size and form *Rhizobium Frankii*, var. *majus*. They were somewhat smaller, end spores less distinct, and the majority were motile during their early life history. They multiplied from spores as well as by transverse division. Their motility was especially noticeable in liquid media, often when of quite mature growth. Sometimes two or even more which had just completed division moved about with great rapidity. Their manner of movement led to the supposition that they possessed cilia. Staining heavily with Hoffman's violet and examining under a Zeiss' homogeneous immersion objective demonstrated the presence of cilia. Each motile organism generally possessed two cilia, one at either end, sometimes only one. Spores just beginning development sometimes had as many as three or four.

Tubes containing culture medium (acid) of stems and leaves of Melilotus showed no development of any kind for eight or ten days, when a small glistening colorless growth was noticed in several of them. Examination showed the presence of much modified *Rhizobium mutabile*. (Plate III, 5.) Cultures renewed from these tubes produced no further developments. In fact all growth ceased shortly in all tubes containing the extract of stems and leaves. The medium was no doubt too acid in reaction. Further efforts with various acid and alkaline media to secure pure cultures of *Rhizobium mutabile* were apparently unsuccessful. Careful examinations of tubercles and cultures obtained from them finally led to the following conclusions:

Tubercles of *Melilotus alba* contain two predominating types of Rhizobia, namely, *Rhizobium Mutabile* and the above described motile forms. These motile forms develop much more readily and by their great numbers prevent the subsequent development of *Rhizobium mutabile*. In the living plant cells the motile Rhizobia are found in the *Infektionsfäden* of Frank. They develop first and by their irritating presence cause the development of the *Fäden* which now are a means of separating the organisms from the other cell contents. This also explains the predominating presence of Rhizobia of *Fäden* in the meristem area of the tubercle. The motion of these Rhizobia is in the direction of their longer axis, hence the tubes (*Fäden*) are produced in the direction of the greatest expenditure of energy. As already stated the irritation caused by their motion induces the cell cytoplasm to deposit around them a coating of cellulose which gives the appearance of *Fäden*. These are found especially in the meristem area; but since the tubercles grow and the *Fäden* are as permanent a structure as the cell wall, they remain as tubes containing spores and mature Rhizobia. The Rhizobia are always found in a position parallel to the long axis of the *Fäden*, except where those peculiar bulgings and swellings occur. Staining the *Fäden* with chlorzinc-iodine showed the presence of a wall containing cellulose. Placing them in various culture media produced no growth or change of any kind; but the contained Rhizobia rapidly developed without producing any continuation of the *Fäden*. This demonstrated that the *Rhizobia* were not the cause of the development of the *Fäden* and that the *Fäden* are not living organisms. After the infected cells of the tubercle had become more mature, the second predominating type of Rhizobium, namely, *Rhiziobium mutabile*, began to develop and finally filled the entire cell. Some tubercles, especially the older ones contain, beside the predominating types, five or six other species. Since these seem to be the conditions of affairs, it can readily be understood how difficult it would be to obtain a pure culture.

It not being practicable to secure a pure culture of *Rhizobium mutabile* of *Melilotus alba*, the next attempt was to secure a pure culture of *Rhizobium Frankii*, var. *majus*, of *Phaseolus vulgaris* (garden bean), but here much the same difficulty was found. Bean tubercles contain also the above described motile form (*Rhizobium Frankii*) in small numbers. However, in order not to lose any more time, and supposing that any species of Rhizobium would serve much the same purpose for these preliminary experiments, bean Rhizobia cultures were continued. They readily grew upon bean-agar extracts and also upon mixtures of corn and bean extracts. It was supposed that they would also grow in pure corn-agar extracts. The question for solution was, How long will it be necessary to allow the Rhizobia to grow in corn-agar extract until they become sufficiently modified to develop in or upon corn roots? The purpose in passing the Rhizobia through a series of culture media made from corn-bean-agar extracts was to modify them gradually, else they might finally die out, if too long continued or suddenly transferred upon pure corn-agar extract. Though the Rhizobia developed upon pure corn root-agar extract, yet it was plainly seen that they grew much better in bean-agar extracts. After the Rhizobia were passed through the series of cultures they were placed in pure corn root-agar extract, a transfer being made every sixth day.

In one month from the time cultures were begun upon the pure corn extract, the first trial inoculations were made upon corn and oats plants which had been grown under the following conditions: Lemonade tumblers of heavy glass (large size) were obtained. A small hole was drilled through the bottom of each for drainage purposes. These were thoroughly washed and sterilized. In the bottom of each was placed a plug of cotton followed by one-half a gill of coarse gravel, then another plug of cotton followed by one-half a kilogram (about one pound) of carefully washed, tertiary quartz sand. The sand in the vessels was then moistened with distilled water. The vessels, with contents, were then placed in a hot air sterilizer for two hours at a temperature of 120° F. After the vessels were sufficiently cool they were planted with sterilized corn (white dent) and oats and placed on a table in the laboratory room. All the seed planted came up in about four days. Some plants were inoculated as soon as they appeared above the sand. Others eleven days after sprouting. Inoculations were made by mixing contents of test tubes containing modified Rhizobia with distilled water and pouring contents over the sand near the stems of the plants, so as to allow as much of the fluid as possible to drain along roots and rootlets. About twenty days after inoculation roots were washed and examined. No tubercles were visible. Inoculated plants of corn looked slightly more thrifty than those not inoculated and possessed more fine rootlets. No other differences were visible to the naked eye. Microscopic examination showed, furthermore, that inoculated corn plants were infected by *Rhizobium Frankii*, var. *majus*. (Plate III, 1.) Infection was by no means general. Some of the hair cells were infected, often causing them to bulge at points of infection. Some of the epidermal cells were infected. The most extensive infection took place in parenchyma cells near the vicinity of secondary root formations, without, however, producing any change in the size and form of the cells. Cells were only partially filled with Rhizobia, as seen in the plate. Inoculated corn plants also possessed more hair cells than those not inoculated. No change whatever was noticeable in oat plants.

The reader will please bear in mind that this is a preliminary report only, and that the results of the experiments are far from being conclusive. The following are, however, the probable conclusions from the apparent results obtained

1. Rhizobia of Leguminosae are capable of being sufficiently modified to develop to a certain extent in root cells of corn (*Zea Mays*).

2. Presence of modified Rhizobia produces increased nutritive changes in corn.

3. Presence of modified Rhizobia (modified in corn root-agar extract) has no visible effect upon oats (*Avena sativa*).

BIBLIOGRAPHY.

Most of the references given in the appended list are to books and pamphlets in the library of the Agricultural Experiment Station of the University of Illinois.   The list, though not complete, gives the references to the most important treatises touching on the subject of Rhizobia and symbiosis.   Starred references are to abstracts or brief reviews.   Other references are to original articles.

André, Ann. Chim. et Phys., 6 ser., 1887.
André, Compt. rend., p. 189, 1891.
*André, Exp. Sta. Record, U. S. Dept. Agr., 1892.
Armsby, Penn. Sta. Ann. Report. p. 195, 1889.
*Armsby, Exp. Sta. Record, U. S. Dept. Agr., 1892.
Atkinson, Bull. Ala. Agr. Sta. No. 9, 1889.
Atkinson, Bull. Tor. Bot. Club, June, 1892.
Atkinson, Bot. Gazette, May, June, July, 1893.
*Atkinson, Hedwigia, Heft 4, 1893.
Atwater, Storrs Agr. School, Conn. Sta., 1889, 1890.
*Atwater, Exp. Sta. Record U. S. Dept. Agr., 1890, 1891, 1892.
Bertholet, Ann. de Chim. t. 13, 14, 1888.
Bertholet, Ann. de Chim., 1889; Nov., 1893.
Bertholet, Compt. rend., p. 543, 1889; p. 842, 1893.
*Bertholet, Bot. Ztg., 1890.
*Bertholet, Exp. Sta. Record, U. S. Dept. Agr., 1891, 1892, 1893.
Beyerinck, Bot. Ztg. No. 46-49-50, 1888.
Beyerinck, Akad. d. Wissensch. Amsterdam, 1890.
Beyerinck, Bot. Ztg. No. 52, 1890.
*Beyerinck, Bot. Centralbl., 1891.
Bivona, Pugill. plant. var. siculae, IV, 26, ——
Bolley, Agr. Science, Vol. VII, No. 2, 1892.
Bornet, Ann. d. Sc. Nat., 5 ser., t. XVII, ——
Bouché, Bot. Ztg., 1852.
Breal, Annales Agronomiques, 1888.
Breal, Compt. rend., Oct. 28, 1889.
*Breal, Bot. Jahresbericht, 1891.
*Breal, Exp. Sta. Record, U. S. Dept. Agr., 1892.
Brefeld, Bot. Untersuchungen, 1883.
Brunchorst, Ber. d. deutsch. bot. Ges., 1885.
Brunchorst, Unters. Bot. Inst. Tüb., ——
Buckhout, Penn. Sta. Ann. Report, 1889.
*Buckhout, Exp. Sta. Record, U. S. Dept. Agr., 1892.
Buscalioni, Malpighia I, 1887.
Clos, Ann. d. Sc. Nat. Bot., 1849.
Cohn, Beiträge zur Biologie, 1876.
Conn, Exp. Sta. Record, U.S. Dept. Agr., 1891, 1892.

Cornu, Memoirs d. l'Acad. d. Sc., 1878.
Cornu, Phylloxera, p. 159, 1878.
de Bary, Die Erscheinung der Symbiose, 1879.
de Condolle, Memoir sur les Legumineuses, 1825.
de Condolle, Prodromus Syst. Nat. Rég. Veg., 1825.
de Vries, Landw. Jahrbücher, S. 233, 933, 1877.
de Vries, Landw. Jahrbücher, IV, 1877.
Descaisne, Traité de Bot. Generale, ——
Douliet, Bull. Soc. Bot. de France, Mai, 1888.
*Douliet, Ann. Agronomiques, 1888.
Ericksson, Acta Universitatis Lund., 1873.
Ericksson, Studier öfver Legnmin Rothk., Lund., 1874.
*Ericksson, Bot. Ztg., 1874.
Frank, Bot. Ztg., No. 24 and 25, 1879.
Frank, Ber. d. deutsch. bot. Ges., Heft 4, 11, 1885.
Frank, Unters. Bot. Inst. Tüb. II, 1886.
Frank, Deutsche Landw. Presse, 1886.
Frank, Krankheiten der Pflanzen, ——
Frank, Ber. d. deutsch. bot. Ges., Heft 1, 8, 10. 1887.
Frank, Ernährung der Pflanzen mit Stickstoff, 1888.
Frank, Ber. d. deutsch. bot. Ges., Heft 2, 3, 1888.
Frank, Ber. d. deutsch. bot. Ges., S. LXXXVII, 1888.
Frank, Ber. d. deutsch. bot. Ges., Heft 1, 5, 1889.
Frank, Landw. Jahrbücher, 1890, 1892.
Frank, Lehrbuch, der Pflanzen physiologie, 1890.
Frank, Pilz-symbiose der Leguminosen, 1890.
Frank, Ber. d. deutsch, bot. Ges., 1891, 1892.
Frank, Lehrbuch der Botanik, 1892.
Frank, Deut. Landw. Presse, No. 19, 1893.
*Frank, Ann. d. la. Sc. Agr., 1890.
*Frank, Bot. Centralbl., 1891.
*Frank, Hedwigia, 1892.
*Frank, Exp. Sta. Record, U. S. Dept. Agr., 1892, 1893.
Frear, Penn. Sta. Ann. Report, 1889.
*Frear, Exp. Sta. Record, U. S. Dept. Agr., 1892.
Gain, Compt. rend., No. 24, 1893.
*Gain, Exp. Sta. Record, U. S. Dept. Agr., 1893.
Gautier, Bull. Soc. Chim. d. Paris, t. 7, 8, ser. 3, ——
*Gautier, Exp. Sta. Record, U. S. Dept. Agr., 1892.
Gilbert, See Lawes, Rothamsted Memoirs, 1860.
Gilbert, Jour. Roy. Agr. Soc. England, Vol. II, ser. 3, ——
*Gilbert, Ann. Agronomiques, 1888.
*Gilbert, Exp. Sta. Record, U. S. Dept. Agr., 1892.
Gravis, Bull. Soc. Roy. de Belgique, Sept., 1879.
*Gravis, Revue Mycologique, II, 1880.
Hartig, Vollstäu. Naturgesch. d. Först. Kult., ——
Hartig, Anatomie und Phys. d. Pflanzan, 1891.
*Hartig, Bot. Centralbl., S. 350, 1886.
Heiden, Landw. Jahrbücher, 1874.
Hellriegel, Tagebl. d. Naturz. Versamm, 1886.
Hellriegel, Stickstoff nahr. d. Gram. u. Leg., 1888.
Hellriegel, Ber. d. deutsch. bot. Ges., 1889.
*Hellriegel, Ann. Agronomiques, 1890.
*Hellriegel, Exp. Sta. Record, U. S. Dept. Agr., 1892.
Hiltner, See Nobbe, Versuchs-Sta., 1868.

Hiltner, Sächs. Landw. Zeitsch., No. 16, 1893.
Hotter, See Nobbe, Landw. Versuchs-Sta., 1860.
*Hotter, Exp. Sta. Record, U. S. Dept. Agr., 1892.
Ilosvoy, Bot. Jahresbericht, Heft 2, 1891.
Immendorff, Landw. Jahrbücher, Heft 1, 2, 1892.
*Immendorff, Exp. Sta. Record, U. S. Dept. Agr., 1892.
Jessen, Sitzungsber. d. bot. Ver. d. Prov. Br'n'd'b., 1879.
Johow, Pringsh. Jahrbücher f. Botanik, 1885, 1889.
Kamienski, Bot. Ztg., 1881.
Kamienski, Mem. d. la soc. Nat. Cherbourg, 1882.
Kny, Sitzungsber. d. bot. Ver., Brand., 1877, 1878.
Kny, Bot. Ztg., 1879.
*Kny, Bot. Ztg., 1879.
Koch, Bot. Ztg., 1890.
Koch, Fühling's Landw. Ztg. H. 4, 1892.
*Koch, Bot. Centralbl., 1891.
Koenig, Stickstoff Vorrat, 1887.
Kolaczek, Lehrbuch der Botanik, 1856.
Kraus. Journal f. Landw., 1890.
*Kraus, Exp. Sta. Record, U. S. Dept. Agr., 1892.
Kühn, Landw. Versuchs-Sta., 1863.
Lachmann, Land. Mittheil. Poppelsdorf, 1856.
Lachmann, Centralbl. f. Bak. u. Parasit'k., 1858.
*Lachmann, Exp. Sta. Record, U. S. Dept. Agr., 1892.
Laurent, Ann. d. l'Institut Pasteur, 1889, 1891, 1892.
Laurent, Compt. rend, 1890, 1891.
*Laurent, Bot. Centralbl., 1891.
*Laurent, Exp. Sta. Record, U. S. Dept. Agr., 1892, 1893.
Lawes, Rothamsted Memoirs, 1860, 1862, 1863, 1882, 1883, 1887, 1889, 1890.
Lawes, Jour. Roy. Agr. Soc. Eng., Vol. II, ser. 3, ——
*Lawes, Ann. Agronomiques, 1888.
*Lawes, Exp. Sta. Record, U. S. Dept. Agr., 1892.
Lecompte, Bull. d. la Soc. Bot. France, 1888.
Lemaout, Traité Gen. de Bot., ——
Liebscher, Deutsche Landw. Presse, 1893.
Liebscher, Jour. f. Landw., H. 1, 2, 1893.
Lohrer, Inaug. Dissertation, Marburg, 1886.
Ludwig, Ber. d. Comm. f. Flora Deutsch., 1890.
*Ludwig, Ber. d. deutsch. bot. Ges., H. 12, 1890.
Lundström, Bot. Centralbl., 1886.
Lundström, Pflanzanphys. Studien II, Upsala, 1887.
Lundström, Bot. Centralbl., 1888.
Lupton, Ala. Coll. Sta., 1890.
*Lupton, Exp. Sta. Record, U. S. Dept. Agr., 1891.
Magnus, Sitzungsber. d. bot. Ver., Brandenburg, 1879.
Malpighi, Anat. Plantarum, 1687.
Mattiorolo, Malpighi I, 1887.
Meyer, Ber. d. deutsch. bot. Ges., 1886, 1887.
Mollberg, Jenaische Zeietschr. f. Naturwiss., 1884.
Möller, Ber. d. deutsch. bot. Ges., 1885, 1892.
*Möller, Hedwigia, 1892.
Morck, Uber die Formen der Bakterien, 1891.
*Müller, Bot. Centralbl., No. 14, 1886.
Naegeli, Linnaea, 1842.
Newman, Ala. Coll. Sta., Bull. No. 16, 1890.

*Newman, Exp. Sta. Record, U. S. Dept. Agr., 1891.
Nobbe, Landw. Versuchs-Sta., 1868, 1890, 1892.
Nobbe, Sächs. Landw. Zeitschr., 1893.
*Nobbe, Exp. Sta. Record, U. S. Dept. Agr., 1892, 1893.
Otto, Ber. d. deutsch. bot. Ges., 1890.
*Otto, Ann. Agron., 1890.
*Otto, Exp. Sta. Record, U. S. Dept. Agr., 1892.
Pagnoul, Ann. Agron., 1890.
*Pagnoul, Exp. Sta. Record, U. S. Dept. Agr., 1892.
*Petermann, Chem. Centralbl., 1892.
*Petermann, Exp. Sta. Record, U. S. Dept. Agr., 1893.
Phelps, Storrs Agr. School, Conn., 1890.
*Phelps, Exp. Sta. Record, U. S. Dept. Agr., 1892.
Pichi, Atti del Soc. Toscana, Sc. Nat., 1888.
Pickard, Compt. rend., 1892.
*Pickard, Exp. Sta. Record, U. S. Dept. Agr., 1892.
Pirotta, Malpighia, 1888.
Prazmowski, Bull. d. Akad. d. Wiss., Krakan, 1889.
Prazmowski, Landw. Versuchs-Sta., 1890.
*Prazmowski, Bot. Centralbl., 1888.
Prillieux, Ann. d. Sc. Nat., 1856.
Prillieux, Bull. Soc. Bot. France, 1879, 1888.
*Prillieux, Bot. Centralbl., 1891.
Pringsheim, Jahrbücher, XVI, ——
Rautenberg, Landw. Versuchs-Sta., 1863.
Rees, Ber. d. deutsch. bot. Ges., 1885.
Reinke, Flora, 1873.
Reissek, Ueber die Endophyt. d. Pflanzen, 1846.
Salfeld, Deutsch. Landw. Ztg., 1890.
Salfeld, Deutsch. Landw. Presse, 1891.
*Salfeld, Exp. Sta. Record, U. S. Dept. Agr., 1892.
Schacht, Monatsber. d. Berl. Ak. d. Wiss., 1854.
Schindler, Oest. Landw. Wochenbl., 1885.
Schindler, Jour. f. Landw. Henneberg, 1885.
Schlicht, Landw. Jahrbücher, 1889.
Schlicht, Bot. Jahresbericht, 1891.
Schloesing, Compt. rend., 1890, 1891.
Schloesing, Ann. d. l'Institut Pasteur, 1892.
*Schloesing, Bot. Centralbl., 1891.
*Schloesing, Exp. Sta. Record, U. S. Dept. Agr., 1892, 1893.
*Schmid, Exp. Sta. Record, U. S. Dept. Agr., 1892.
Schmid, See Nobbe, Versuchs-Sta., ——
*Schmitter, Exp. Sta. Record, U. S. Dept. Agr., 1892.
Schneider, Bull. Tor. Bot. Club, 1892.
Schneider, Am. Naturalist, Sept., 1893.
*Schneider, Hedwigia, 1892.
*Schneider, Revue Mycologique, 1893.
*Schneider, Bot. Centralbl., 1893.
Schroeter Natürlichen Pflanzanfamilien, 1890.
Schulze, Landw. Jahrbücher, 1890.
Serno, Landw. Jahrbücher, H. 6, 1889.
Sorauer, Pflanzenkrankheiten, 2te. Aufl., 1886.
*Sorauer, Bot. Centralbl., 1887.
Strecker, Jour. f. Landw., 1886.
Thaer, Jour. f. Landw., 1879, 1884.

Tollens, Landw. Versuchs-Sta., 1891.
Treviranus, Bot. Ztg., 1853.
Troschke, Landw. Versuchs-Sta., 1884.
Troschke, Biedermann's Centralbl., 1884.
Troschke, Wochenschr. d. Pomm. Ok. Ges., 1884.
Tschirch, Ber. d. deutsch. bot. Ges., H. 2, 5, 1887.
Tschirch, Centralbl. f. Bak. u. Parasit'k'de., 1887.
Tschirch, Ges. naturw. Freunde, Berlin, 1887.
*Tschirch, Ann. Agron., 1888.
*Tschirch, Forch. auf. d. Gebiete d. Agr., 1888.
Van Beneden, Archives de Biologie, 1880.
*Van Tiegham, Ann. Agron., 1888.
Van Tiegham, Bull. d. la Soc. Bot., 1888.
Vibranes, Deutsche Landw. Presse, 1893.
Vines, Ann. of Bot., 1888, 1889.
Vogel, Jour. f. Landw., 1890.
Vuillemin, Jour. d. Bot.. 1888.
Vuillemin, Ann. d. Sc. Agr., 1888.
Wahrlich, Bot. Ztg., 1886.
Ward, Phil. Transac. Roy. Soc., London, 1887.
Ward, Ann. of Bot., 1888.
Ward, Proceedings Roy. Soc., London, 1889.
*Ward, Biedermann's Centralbl., 1888.
*Ward, Ann. Sc. Agron., 1888.
Warington, U. S. Exp. Sta., Bull. No. 8, 1892.
*Warington, Exp. Sta. Record, U. S. Dept. Agr., 1892
Warming, Bot. Jahresber., 1876.
Weber, Bot. Ztg., 1884.
Wigand, Forch. a. d. bot. Gar. z. Marburg, 1887.
Willfarth, Beilageh. z. Rübenz. Indus., Nov., 1888.
Willfarth, Deutsche Landw. Rundschau, Nos. 8, 9, 10, 11, 1892.
*Willfarth, Ann. Agron., 1888.
*Willfarth, Bot. Centralbl., 1889.
*Willfarth, Chem. Centralbl., 1893.
*Willfarth, Exp. Sta. Record, U. S. Dept. Agr., 1893.
Wittmack, Verh. d. Bot. Ver., Brandenburg, 1874.
Wolff, Brand des Getreides, 1874.
Woods, Storrs Agr. School, Bull. No. 5, 1889,
Woods, Storrs Agr. School, Conn., p. 44, Rep't, 1890.
*Woods, Exp. Sta. Record, U. S. Dept. Agr., 1890, 1891, 1892
Woronin, Mém. d. l'Acad. d. Sc., No. 6, 1866.
Woronin, Ann. sc. nat., 1867.
Woronin, Pringsheim's Jahrbücher, 1877, 1878.
Woronin, Ber. d. deutsch. bot. Ges., 1885.
Woronin, Mém. Acad. Imp. d. Sc., 1886.
*Woronin, Bot. Centralbl., 1889.
Zopf, Die Pilze, 1890.

ALBERT SCHNEIDER.

EXPLANATION OF PLATES.

PLATE I. —1. Longitudinal median section of portion of rootlet and developing tubercle of *Trifolium Pratense*. (*a*) Normal hair cells. (*b*) Hair cell infected by Rhizobia. (*c*) Dwarfed hair cells on tubercle. (*d*) Epidermal layer. (*e*) Infected area of tubercle. Cells are enlarged containing Rhizobia, *Infektionsfäden*, and abnormally large nuclei. (*f*) *Infektionsfäden* containing smaller Rhizobia. (*Rhizobium Frankii?*). (Left colorless in this figure). (*g*) Apical area of tubercle. Subsequent development of the tubercle is outward from this area. (*h*) Area from which the vascular system of the tubercle will arise. (*i*) Vascular system of rootlet.

2. Semidiagramatic figures showing probable mode of the growth and extension of the *Infektionsfäden* in the infected area of tubercle.

I. Single cell from the apical area of tubercle. (*a*) The beginning of an *Infektionsfäden*. It is simply a group of Rhizobia surrounded by a coating of cellulose secreted by the cell cytoplasm. (*b*) Another group of Rhizobia differing from those of (*a*). They freely mix with the cell cytoplasm and do not have a coating of cellulose deposited around them. (Example, *Rhizobium mutabile.*) (*n*) Neuclus of cell.

II. Later stage of the same cell. Groups (*a*) and (*b*) are enlarged. The nucleus has begun to divide.

III. Later stage than II. The new cell wall (*c*) has begun to form, passing through both groups of Rhizobia.

IV. Complete cell division. Two autoinfected daughter cells have developed from the mother cell. As is seen, the *Fäden* are not of the same thickness throughout. Local increase in the development of Rhizobia causes swellings. This is nearly always the case next to the new cell wall (III and IV).

V. Group of mature cells from infected area. (*a*) *Infektionsfäden* filled with Rhizobia (*Rhizobium Frankii?*). (*b*) *Rhizobium mutabile* filling remaining portion of cell and intimately mixed with cell cytoplasm forming the mycoplasm of of Brunchorst and Frank.

3. Small portion of root of *Melilotus alba* with tubercles. (*a*) Developing tubercles. (*b*) Later stage showing dichotomous mode of branching of tubercle. (*c*) Single mature tubercles. (*d*) Grape bunch-like group of tubercles. Very common with Melilotus.

[1 and 2, highly magnified; 3 is natural size.]

PLATE II.—1. Peculiar Rhizobia sparingly present in infected cells of tubercles of *Petalostemon violaceus*. As a rule, each cell contains three or four of these organisms.

2. *Rhizobium mutabile* of Trifolium (clover). (*a*) Spores. (*b*) Developing spores.

3. *Rhizobium mutabile* of *Melilotus alba* (sweet clover). (*a*) and (*b*) as in 2.

4. *Rhizobium mutabile* of Trifolium, later stage.

5. *Rhizobium curvum* of Phaseolus (bean).

6. *Rhizobium Frankii*, var. *majus*, of *Phaseolus vulgaris.*

7. *Rhizobium Frankii* of Infektionsfäden of Melilotus, Trifolium, and other genera of plants.

8. *Rhizobium Frankii*, var. *minus* of Pisum (pea) *Infektionsfäden*. (*a*) Spores and young Rhizobia with cilia.

9. *Rhizobium spheroides* of *Pisum sativum.* They often contain highly refractive bodies the function of which is undetermined.

10. *Rhizobium nodosum* of Cassia (partridge pea).

[Highly magnified.]

PLATE III.—1. Longitudinal section of portions of inoculated corn (*Zea Mays*) rootlet. (*a*) Hair cells infected by modified Rhizobia. Cells become somewhat enlarged at points of infection. (*b*) Parenchyma cells infected by modified Rhizobia; cells remain unchanged. (*c*) Secondary rootlet.

2. *Rhizobium mutabile* cultivated upon bean and corn root extract.

3. *Rhizobium mutabile* cultivated upon corn root extract.

4. *Rhizobium mutabile* cultivated upon sweet clover root extract.

5. *Rhizobium mutabile* cultivated upon sweet clover extract prepared from stems and leaves.

All culture media were solidified by agar-agar.

[Highly magnified.]

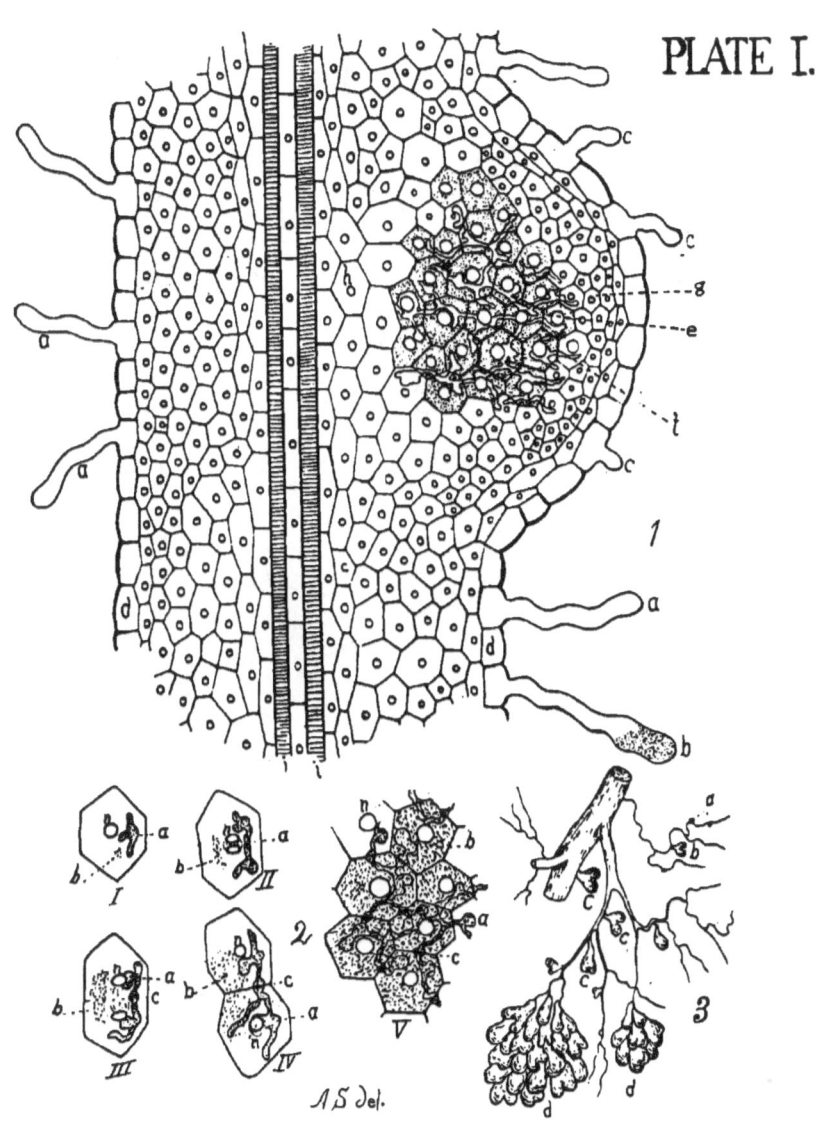

PLATE I.

PLATE II.

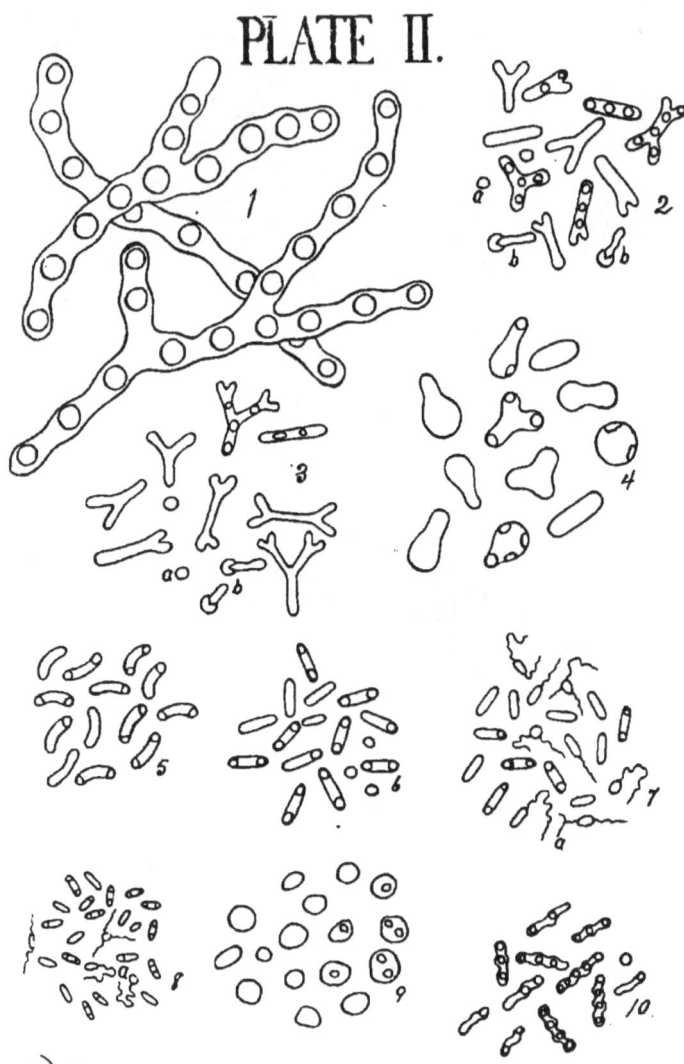

A. S. del

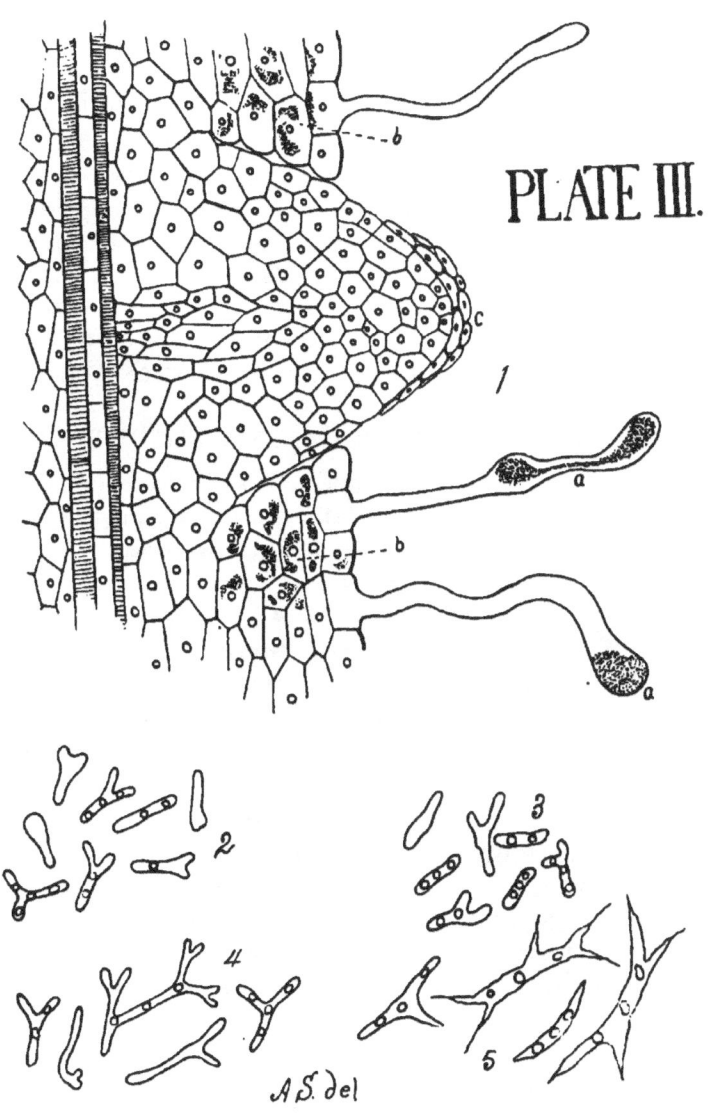

PLATE III.

ORGANIZATION.